Anna Christie

Eugene O'Neill

Anna Christie

The present edition is a reproduction of previous publication of this classic work. Minor typographical errors may have been corrected without note; however, for an authentic reading experience the spelling, punctuation, and capitalization have been retained from the original text.

ISBN: 978-1-63637-935-7

CONTENTS

"ANNA CHRISTIE"

A PLAY IN FOUR ACTS

CHARACTERS

"JOHNNY-THE-PRIEST"

TWO LONGSHOREMEN

A POSTMAN

LARRY, bartender

CHRIS. CHRISTOPHERSON, captain of the barge "Simeon Winthrop"

MARTHY OWEN

ANNA CHRISTOPHERSON, Chris's daughter

THREE MEN OF A STEAMER'S CREW

MAT BURKE, a stoker

JOHNSON, deckhand on the barge

Time of the Play—About 1910

1

ACT I

SCENE—"Johnny-The-Priest's" saloon near South Street, New York City. The stage is divided into two sections, showing a small back room on the right. On the left, forward, of the barroom, a large window looking out on the street. Beyond it, the main entrance—a double swinging door. Farther back, another window. The bar runs from left to right nearly the whole length of the rear wall. In back of the bar, a small showcase displaying a few bottles of case goods, for which there is evidently little call. The remainder of the rear space in front of the large mirrors is occupied by half-barrels of cheap whiskey of the "nickel-a-shot" variety, from which the liquor is drawn by means of spigots. On the right is an open doorway leading to the back room. In the back room are four round wooden tables with five chairs grouped about each. In the rear, a family entrance opening on a side street.

It is late afternoon of a day in fall.

As the curtain rises, Johnny is discovered. "Johnny-The-Priest" deserves his nickname. With his pale, thin, clean-shaven face, mild blue eyes and white hair, a cassock would seem more suited to him than the apron he wears. Neither his voice nor his general manner dispel this illusion which has made him a personage of the water front. They are soft and bland. But beneath all his mildness one senses the man behind the mask—cynical, callous, hard as nails. He is lounging at ease behind the bar, a pair of spectacles on his nose, reading an evening paper.

Two longshoremen enter from the street, wearing their working aprons, the button of the union pinned conspicuously on the caps pulled sideways on their heads at an aggressive angle.

FIRST LONGSHOREMAN—[As they range themselves at the bar.] Gimme a shock. Number Two. [He tosses a coin on the bar.]

SECOND LONGSHOREMAN—Same here. [Johnny sets two glasses of barrel whiskey before them.]

FIRST LONGSHOREMAN—Here's luck! [The other nods. They gulp down their whiskey.]

SECOND LONGSHOREMAN—[Putting money on the bar.] Give us another.

FIRST LONGSHOREMAN—Gimme a scoop this time—lager and porter. I'm dry.

SECOND LONGSHOREMAN—Same here. [Johnny draws the lager and porter and sets the big, foaming schooners before them. They drink down half the contents and start to talk together hurriedly in low tones. The door on the left is swung open and Larry enters. He is a boyish, red-cheeked, rather good-looking young fellow of twenty or so.]

LARRY—[Nodding to Johnny—cheerily.] Hello, boss.

JOHNNY—Hello, Larry. [With a glance at his watch.] Just on time. [LARRY goes to the right behind the bar, takes off his coat, and puts on an apron.]

FIRST LONGSHOREMAN—[Abruptly.] Let's drink up and get back to it. [They finish their drinks and go out left. The POSTMAN enters as they leave. He exchanges nods with JOHNNY and throws a letter on the bar.]

THE POSTMAN—Addressed care of you, Johnny. Know him?

JOHNNY—[Picks up the letter, adjusting his spectacles. LARRY comes and peers over his shoulders. JOHNNY reads very slowly.] Christopher Christopherson.

THE POSTMAN—[Helpfully.] Square-head name.

3

LARRY—Old Chris—that's who.

JOHNNY—Oh, sure. I was forgetting Chris carried a hell of a name like that. Letters come here for him sometimes before, I remember now. Long time ago, though.

THE POSTMAN—It'll get him all right then?

JOHNNY—Sure thing. He comes here whenever he's in port.

THE POSTMAN—[Turning to go.] Sailor, eh?

JOHNNY—[With a grin.] Captain of a coal barge.

THE POSTMAN—[Laughing.] Some job! Well, s'long.

JOHNNY—S'long. I'll see he gets it. [The POSTMAN goes out. JOHNNY scrutinizes the letter.] You got good eyes, Larry. Where's it from?

LARRY—[After a glance.] St. Paul. That'll be in Minnesota, I'm thinkin'. Looks like a woman's writing, too, the old divil!
JOHNNY—He's got a daughter somewheres out West, I think he told me once. [He puts the letter on the cash register.] Come to think of it, I ain't seen old Chris in a dog's age. [Putting his overcoat on, he comes around the end of the bar.] Guess I'll be gettin' home. See you to-morrow.

LARRY—Good-night to ye, boss. [As JOHNNY goes toward the street door, it is pushed open and CHRISTOPHER CHRISTOPHERSON enters. He is a short, squat, broad-shouldered man of about fifty, with a round, weather-beaten, red face from which his light blue eyes peer short-sightedly, twinkling with a simple good humor. His large mouth, overhung by a thick, drooping, yellow mustache, is childishly self-willed and weak, of an obstinate kindliness. A thick neck is jammed like a post into the heavy trunk of his body. His arms with their big, hairy, freckled hands, and his stumpy legs terminating in large flat feet, are awkwardly short and muscular. He walks with a clumsy, rolling gait. His voice, when not raised in a hollow boom, is toned down to

4

a sly, confidential half-whisper with something vaguely plaintive in its quality. He is dressed in a wrinkled, ill-fitting dark suit of shore clothes, and wears a faded cap of gray cloth over his mop of grizzled, blond hair. Just now his face beams with a too-blissful happiness, and he has evidently been drinking. He reaches his hand out to JOHNNY.]

CHRIS—Hello, Yohnny! Have drink on me. Come on, Larry. Give us drink. Have one yourself. [Putting his hand in his pocket.] Ay gat money—plenty money.

JOHNNY—[Shakes CHRIS by the hand.] Speak of the devil. We was just talkin' about you.

LARRY—[Coming to the end of the bar.] Hello, Chris. Put it there. [They shake hands.]

CHRIS—[Beaming.] Give us drink.

JOHNNY—[With a grin.] You got a half-snootful now. Where'd you get it?

CHRIS—[Grinning.] Oder fallar on oder barge—Irish fallar—he gat bottle vhiskey and we drank it, yust us two. Dot vhiskey gat kick, by yingo! Ay yust come ashore. Give us drink, Larry. Ay vas little drunk, not much. Yust feel good. [He laughs and commences to sing in a nasal, high-pitched quaver.]

"My Yosephine, come board de ship. Long time Ay vait for you.
De moon, she shi-i-i-ine. She looka yust like you.
Tchee-tchee, tchee-tchee, tchee-tchee, tchee-tchee."

[To the accompaniment of this last he waves his hand as if he were conducting an orchestra.]

JOHNNY—[With a laugh.] Same old Yosie, eh, Chris?

CHRIS—You don't know good song when you hear him. Italian

5

fallar on oder barge, he learn me dat. Give us drink. [He throws change on the bar.]

LARRY—[With a professional air.] What's your pleasure, gentlemen?

JOHNNY—Small beer, Larry.

CHRIS—Vhiskey—Number Two.

LARRY—[As he gets their drinks.] I'll take a cigar on you.

CHRIS—[Lifting his glass.] Skoal! [He drinks.]

JOHNNY—Drink hearty.

CHRIS—[Immediately.] Have oder drink.

JOHNNY—No. Some other time. Got to go home now. So you've just landed? Where are you in from this time?

CHRIS—Norfolk. Ve make slow voyage—dirty vedder—yust fog, fog, fog, all bloody time! [There is an insistent ring from the doorbell at the family entrance in the back room. Chris gives a start—hurriedly.] Ay go open, Larry. Ay forgat. It vas Marthy. She come with me. [He goes into the back room.]

LARRY—[With a chuckle.] He's still got that same cow livin' with him, the old fool!

JOHNNY—[With a grin.] A sport, Chris is. Well, I'll beat it home. S'long. [He goes to the street door.]

LARRY—So long, boss.

JOHNNY—Oh—don't forget to give him his letter.

LARRY—I won't. [JOHNNY goes out. In the meantime, CHRIS has opened the family entrance door, admitting MARTHY. She might be forty or fifty. Her jowly, mottled face, with its thick red nose, is streaked with interlacing purple veins. Her thick, gray hair is piled

6

anyhow in a greasy mop on top of her round head. Her figure is flabby and fat; her breath comes in wheezy gasps; she speaks in a loud, mannish voice, punctuated by explosions of hoarse laughter. But there still twinkles in her blood-shot blue eyes a youthful lust for life which hard usage has failed to stifle, a sense of humor mocking, but good-tempered. She wears a man's cap, double-breasted man's jacket, and a grimy, calico skirt. Her bare feet are encased in a man's brogans several sizes too large for her, which gives her a shuffling, wobbly gait.]

MARTHY—[Grumblingly.] What yuh tryin' to do, Dutchy—keep me standin' out there all day? [She comes forward and sits at the table in the right corner, front.]

CHRIS—[Mollifyingly.] Ay'm sorry, Marthy. Ay talk to Yohnny. Ay forgat. What you goin' take for drink?

MARTHY—[Appeased.] Gimme a scoop of lager an' ale.

CHRIS—Ay go bring him back. [He returns to the bar.] Lager and ale for Marthy, Larry. Vhiskey for me. [He throws change on the bar.]

LARRY—Right you are. [Then remembering, he takes the letter from in back of the bar.] Here's a letter for you—from St. Paul, Minnesota—and a lady's writin'. [He grins.]

CHRIS—[Quickly—taking it.] Oh, den it come from my daughter, Anna. She live dere. [He turns the letter over in his hands uncertainly.] Ay don't gat letter from Anna—must be a year.

LARRY—[Jokingly.] That's a fine fairy tale to be tellin'—your daughter! Sure I'll bet it's some bum.

CHRIS—[Soberly.] No. Dis come from Anna. [Engrossed by the letter in his hand—uncertainly.] By golly, Ay tank Ay'm too drunk for read dis letter from Anna. Ay tank Ay sat down for a minute. You bring drinks in back room, Larry. [He goes into the room on right.]

7

MARTHY—[Angrily.] Where's my lager an' ale, yuh big stiff?

CHRIS—[Preoccupied.] Larry bring him. [He sits down opposite her. LARRY brings in the drinks and sets them on the table. He and MARTHY exchange nods of recognition. LARRY stands looking at CHRIS curiously. MARTHY takes a long draught of her schooner and heaves a huge sigh of satisfaction, wiping her mouth with the back of her hand. CHRIS stares at the letter for a moment—slowly opens it, and, squinting his eyes, commences to read laboriously, his lips moving as he spells out the words. As he reads his face lights up with an expression of mingled joy and bewilderment.]

LARRY—Good news?

MARTHY—[Her curiosity also aroused.] What's that yuh got—a letter, fur Gawd's sake?

CHRIS—[Pauses for a moment, after finishing the letter, as if to let the news sink in—then suddenly pounds his fist on the table with happy excitement.] Py yiminy! Yust tank, Anna say she's comin' here right avay! She gat sick on yob in St. Paul, she say. It's short letter, don't tal me much more'n dat. [Beaming.] Py golly, dat's good news all at one time for ole fallar! [Then turning to MARTHY, rather shamefacedly.] You know, Marthy, Ay've tole you Ay don't see my Anna since she vas little gel in Sveden five year ole.

MARTHY—How old'll she be now?

CHRIS—She must be—lat me see—she must be twenty year ole, py Yo!

LARRY—[Surprised.] You've not seen her in fifteen years?

CHRIS—[Suddenly growing somber—in a low tone.] No. Ven she vas little gel, Ay vas bo'sun on vindjammer. Ay never gat home only few time dem year. Ay'm fool sailor fallar. My voman—Anna's mother—she gat tired vait all time Sveden for me ven Ay don't never come. She come dis country, bring Anna, dey go out Minnesota, live with her cousins on farm. Den ven her mo'der die

8

ven Ay vas on voyage, Ay tank it's better dem cousins keep Anna. Ay tank it's better Anna live on farm, den she don't know dat ole davil, sea, she don't know fader like me.

LARRY—[With a wink at MARTHY.] This girl, now, 'll be marryin' a sailor herself, likely. It's in the blood.

CHRIS—[Suddenly springing to his feet and smashing his fist on the table in a rage.] No, py God! She don't do dat!

MARTHY—[Grasping her schooner hastily—angrily.] Hey, look out, yuh nut! Wanta spill my suds for me?

LARRY—[Amazed.] Oho, what's up with you? Ain't you a sailor yourself now, and always been?

CHRIS—[Slowly.] Dat's yust vhy Ay say it. [Forcing a smile.] Sailor vas all right fallar, but not for marry gel. No. Ay know dat. Anna's mo'der, she know it, too.

LARRY—[As CHRIS remains sunk in gloomy reflection.] When is your daughter comin'? Soon?

CHRIS—[Roused.] Py yiminy, Ay forgat. [Reads through the letter hurriedly.] She say she come right avay, dat's all.

LARRY—She'll maybe be comin' here to look for you, I s'pose. [He returns to the bar, whistling. Left alone with MARTHY, who stares at him with a twinkle of malicious humor in her eyes, CHRIS suddenly becomes desperately ill-at-ease. He fidgets, then gets up hurriedly.]

CHRIS—Ay gat speak with Larry. Ay be right back. [Mollifyingly.] Ay bring you oder drink.

MARTHY—[Emptying her glass.] Sure. That's me. [As he retreats with the glass she guffaws after him derisively.]

CHRIS—[To LARRY in an alarmed whisper.] Py yingo, Ay gat gat

9

Marthy shore off barge before Anna come! Anna raise hell if she find dat out. Marthy raise hell, too, for go, py golly!

LARRY—[With a chuckle.] Serve ye right, ye old divil—havin' a woman at your age!

CHRIS—[Scratching his head in a quandary.] You tal me lie for tal Marthy, Larry, so's she gat off barge quick.

LARRY—She knows your daughter's comin'. Tell her to get the hell out of it.

CHRIS—No. Ay don't like make her feel bad.

LARRY—You're an old mush! Keep your girl away from the barge, then. She'll likely want to stay ashore anyway. [Curiously.] What does she work at, your Anna?

CHRIS—She stay on dem cousins' farm 'till two year ago. Dan she gat yob nurse gel in St. Paul. [Then shaking his head resolutely.] But Ay don't vant for her gat yob now. Ay vant for her stay with me.

LARRY—[Scornfully.] On a coal barge! She'll not like that, I'm thinkin'.

MARTHY—[Shouts from next room.] Don't I get that bucket o' suds, Dutchy?

CHRIS—[Startled—in apprehensive confusion.] Yes, Ay come, Marthy.

LARRY—[Drawing the lager and ale, hands it to CHRIS— laughing.] Now you're in for it! You'd better tell her straight to get out!

CHRIS—[Shaking in his boots.] Py golly. [He takes her drink in to MARTHY and sits down at the table. She sips it in silence. LARRY moves quietly close to the partition to listen, grinning with expectation. CHRIS seems on the verge of speaking, hesitates, gulps

10

down his whiskey desperately as if seeking for courage. He attempts to whistle a few bars of "Yosephine" with careless bravado, but the whistle peters out futilely. MARTHY stares at him keenly, taking in his embarrassment with a malicious twinkle of amusement in her eye. CHRIS clears his throat.] Marthy—

MARTHY—[Aggressively.] Wha's that? [Then, pretending to fly into a rage, her eyes enjoying CHRIS' misery.] I'm wise to what's in back of your nut, Dutchy. Yuh want to git rid o' me, huh?—now she's comin'. Gimme the bum's rush ashore, huh? Lemme tell yuh, Dutchy, there ain't a square-head workin' on a boat man enough to git away with that. Don't start nothin' yuh can't finish!

CHRIS—[Miserably.] Ay don't start nutting, Marthy.

MARTHY—[Glares at him for a second—then cannot control a burst of laughter.] Ho-ho! Yuh're a scream, Square-head—an honest-ter-Gawd knockout! Ho-ho! [She wheezes, panting for breath.]

CHRIS—[With childish pique.] Ay don't see nutting for laugh at.

MARTHY—Take a slant in the mirror and yuh'll see. Ho-ho! [Recovering from her mirth—chuckling, scornfully.] A square-head tryin' to kid Marthy Owen at this late day!—after me campin' with barge men the last twenty years. I'm wise to the game, up, down, and sideways. I ain't been born and dragged up on the water front for nothin'. Think I'd make trouble, huh? Not me! I'll pack up me duds an' beat it. I'm quittin' yuh, get me? I'm tellin' yuh I'm sick of stickin' with yuh, and I'm leavin' yuh flat, see? There's plenty of other guys on other barges waitin' for me. Always was, I always found. [She claps the astonished CHRIS on the back.] So cheer up, Dutchy! I'll be offen the barge before she comes. You'll be rid o' me for good—and me o' you—good riddance for both of us. Ho-ho!

CHRIS—[Seriously.] Ay don' tank dat. You vas good gel, Marthy.

MARTHY—[Grinning.] Good girl? Aw, can the bull! Well, yuh

11

treated me square, yuhself. So it's fifty-fifty. Nobody's sore at nobody. We're still good frien's, huh? [LARRY returns to bar.]

CHRIS—[Beaming now that he sees his troubles disappearing.] Yes, py golly.

MARTHY—That's the talkin'! In all my time I tried never to split with a guy with no hard feelin's. But what was yuh so scared about—that I'd kick up a row? That ain't Marthy's way. [Scornfully.] Think I'd break my heart to lose yuh? Commit suicide, huh? Ho-ho! Gawd! The world's full o' men if that's all I'd worry about! [Then with a grin, after emptying her glass.] Blow me to another scoop, huh? I'll drink your kid's health for yuh.

CHRIS—[Eagerly.] Sure tang. Ay go gat him. [He takes the two glasses into the bar.] Oder drink. Same for both.

LARRY—[Getting the drinks and putting them on the bar.] She's not such a bad lot, that one.

CHRIS—[Jovially.] She's good gel, Ay tal you! Py golly, Ay calabrate now! Give me vhiskey here at bar, too. [He puts down money. LARRY serves him.] You have drink, Larry.

LARRY—[Virtuously.] You know I never touch it.

CHRIS—You don't know what you miss. Skoal! [He drinks—then begins to sing loudly.]

"My Yosephine, come board de ship—"

[He picks up the drinks for MARTHY and himself and walks unsteadily into the back room, singing.]

"De moon, she shi-i-ine. She looks yust like you.
Tche-tchee, tchee-tchee, tchee-tchee, tchee-tchee."

MARTHY—[Grinning, hands to ears.] Gawd!

CHRIS—[Sitting down.] Ay'm good singer, yes? Ve drink, eh?

12

Skoal! Ay calabrate! [He drinks.] Ay calabrate 'cause Anna's coming home. You know, Marthy, Ay never write for her to come, 'cause Ay tank Ay'm no good for her. But all time Ay hope like hell some day she vant for see me and den she come. And dat's vay it happen now, py yiminy! [His face beaming.] What you tank she look like, Marthy? Ay bet you she's fine, good, strong gel, pooty like hell! Living on farm made her like dat. And Ay bet you some day she marry good, steady land fallar here in East, have home all her own, have kits—and dan Ay'm ole grandfader, py golly! And Ay go visit dem every time Ay gat in port near! [Bursting with joy.] By yiminy crickens, Ay calabrate dat! [Shouts.] Bring oder drink, Larry! [He smashes his fist on the table with a bang.]

LARRY—[Coming in from bar—irritably.] Easy there! Don't be breakin' the table, you old goat!

CHRIS—[By way of reply, grins foolishly and begins to sing.] "My Yosephine comes board de ship—"

MARTHY—[Touching CHRIS' arm persuasively.] You're soused to the ears, Dutchy. Go out and put a feed into you. It'll sober you up. [Then as CHRIS shakes his head obstinately.] Listen, yuh old nut! Yuh don't know what time your kid's liable to show up. Yuh want to be sober when she comes, don't yuh?

CHRIS—[Aroused—gets unsteadily to his feet.] Py golly, yes.

LARRY—That's good sense for you. A good beef stew'll fix you. Go round the corner.

CHRIS—All right. Ay be back soon, Marthy. [CHRIS goes through the bar and out the street door.]

LARRY—He'll come round all right with some grub in him.

MARTHY—Sure. [LARRY goes back to the bar and resumes his newspaper. MARTHY sips what is left of her schooner reflectively. There is the ring of the family entrance bell. LARRY comes to the door and opens it a trifle—then, with a puzzled expression, pulls it

13

wide. ANNA CHRISTOPHERSON enters. She is a tall, blond, fully-developed girl of twenty, handsome after a large, Viking-daughter fashion but now run down in health and plainly showing all the outward evidences of belonging to the world's oldest profession. Her youthful face is already hard and cynical beneath its layer of make-up. Her clothes are the tawdry finery of peasant stock turned prostitute. She comes and sinks wearily in a chair by the table, left front.]

ANNA—Gimme a whiskey—ginger ale on the side. [Then, as LARRY turns to go, forcing a winning smile at him.] And don't be stingy, baby.

LARRY—[Sarcastically.] Shall I serve it in a pail?

ANNA—[With a hard laugh.] That suits me down to the ground. [LARRY goes into the bar. The two women size each other up with frank stares. LARRY comes back with the drink which he sets before ANNA and returns to the bar again. ANNA downs her drink at a gulp. Then, after a moment, as the alcohol begins to rouse her, she turns to MARTHY with a friendly smile.] Gee, I needed that bad, all right, all right!

MARTHY—[Nodding her head sympathetically.] Sure—yuh look all in. Been on a bat?

ANNA—No—travelling—day and a half on the train. Had to sit up all night in the dirty coach, too. Gawd, I thought I'd never get here!

MARTHY—[With a start—looking at her intently.] Where'd yuh come from, huh?

ANNA—St. Paul—out in Minnesota.

MARTHY—[Staring at her in amazement—slowly.] So—yuh're—[She suddenly bursts out into hoarse, ironical laughter.] Gawd!

ANNA—All the way from Minnesota, sure. [Flaring up.] What you laughing at? Me?

14

MARTHY—[Hastily.] No, honest, kid. I was thinkin' of somethin' else.

ANNA—[Mollified—with a smile.] Well, I wouldn't blame you, at that. Guess I do look rotten—yust out of the hospital two weeks. I'm going to have another 'ski. What d'you say? Have something on me?

MARTHY—Sure I will. T'anks. [She calls.] Hey, Larry! Little service! [He comes in.]

ANNA—Same for me.

MARTHY—Same here. [LARRY takes their glasses and goes out.]

ANNA—Why don't you come sit over here, be sociable. I'm a dead stranger in this burg—and I ain't spoke a word with no one since day before yesterday.

MARTHY—Sure thing. [She shuffles over to ANNA'S table and sits down opposite her. LARRY brings the drinks and ANNA pays him.]

ANNA—Skoal! Here's how! [She drinks.]

MARTHY—Here's luck! [She takes a gulp from her schooner.]

ANNA—[Taking a package of Sweet Caporal cigarettes from her bag.] Let you smoke in here, won't they?

MARTHY—[Doubtfully.] Sure. [Then with evident anxiety.] On'y trow it away if yuh hear someone comin'.

ANNA—[Lighting one and taking a deep inhale.] Gee, they're fussy in this dump, ain't they? [She puffs, staring at the table top. MARTHY looks her over with a new penetrating interest, taking in every detail of her face. ANNA suddenly becomes conscious of this appraising stare—resentfully.] Ain't nothing wrong with me, is there? You're looking hard enough.

15

MARTHY—[Irritated by the other's tone—scornfully.] Ain't got to look much. I got your number the minute you stepped in the door.

ANNA—[Her eyes narrowing.] Ain't you smart! Well, I got yours, too, without no trouble. You're me forty years from now. That's you! [She gives a hard little laugh.]

MARTHY—[Angrily.] Is that so? Well, I'll tell you straight, kiddo, that Marthy Owen never—[She catches herself up short—with a grin.] What are you and me scrappin' over? Let's cut it out, huh? Me, I don't want no hard feelin's with no one. [Extending her hand.] Shake and forget it, huh?

ANNA—[Shakes her hand gladly.] Only too glad to. I ain't looking for trouble. Let's have 'nother. What d'you say?

MARTHY—[Shaking her head.] Not for mine. I'm full up. And you— Had anythin' to eat lately?

ANNA—Not since this morning on the train.

MARTHY—Then yuh better go easy on it, hadn't yuh?

ANNA—[After a moment's hesitation.] Guess you're right. I got to meet someone, too. But my nerves is on edge after that rotten trip.

MARTHY—Yuh said yuh was just outa the hospital?

ANNA—Two weeks ago. [Leaning over to MARTHY confidentially.] The joint I was in out in St. Paul got raided. That was the start. The judge give all us girls thirty days. The others didn't seem to mind being in the cooler much. Some of 'em was used to it. But me, I couldn't stand it. It got my goat right—couldn't eat or sleep or nothing. I never could stand being caged up nowheres. I got good and sick and they had to send me to the hospital. It was nice there. I was sorry to leave it, honest!

MARTHY—[After a slight pause.] Did yuh say yuh got to meet someone here?

16

ANNA—Yes. Oh, not what you mean. It's my Old Man I got to meet. Honest! It's funny, too. I ain't seen him since I was a kid—don't even know what he looks like—yust had a letter every now and then. This was always the only address he give me to write him back. He's yanitor of some building here now—used to be a sailor.

MARTHY—[Astonished.] Janitor!

ANNA—Sure. And I was thinking maybe, seeing he ain't never done a thing for me in my life, he might be willing to stake me to a room and eats till I get rested up. [Wearily.] Gee, I sure need that rest! I'm knocked out. [Then resignedly.] But I ain't expecting much from him. Give you a kick when you're down, that's what all men do. [With sudden passion.] Men, I hate 'em—all of 'em! And I don't expect he'll turn out no better than the rest. [Then with sudden interest.] Say, do you hang out around this dump much?

MARTHY—Oh, off and on.

ANNA—Then maybe you know him—my Old Man—or at least seen him?

MARTHY—It ain't old Chris, is it?

ANNA—Old Chris?

MARTHY—Chris Christopherson, his full name is.

ANNA—[Excitedly.] Yes, that's him! Anna Christopherson—that's my real name—only out there I called myself Anna Christie. So you know him, eh?

MARTHY—[Evasively.] Seen him about for years.

ANNA—Say, what's he like, tell me, honest?

MARTHY—Oh, he's short and—

ANNA—[Impatiently.] I don't care what he looks like. What kind is he?

17

MARTHY—[Earnestly.] Well, yuh can bet your life, kid, he's as good an old guy as ever walked on two feet. That goes!

ANNA—[Pleased.] I'm glad to hear it. Then you think's he'll stake me to that rest cure I'm after?

MARTHY—[Emphatically.] Surest thing you know. [Disgustedly.] But where'd yuh get the idea he was a janitor?

ANNA—He wrote me he was himself.

MARTHY—Well, he was lyin'. He ain't. He's captain of a barge—five men under him.

ANNA—[Disgusted in her turn.] A barge? What kind of a barge?

MARTHY—Coal, mostly.

ANNA—A coal barge! [With a harsh laugh.] If that ain't a swell job to find your long lost Old Man working at! Gee, I knew something'd be bound to turn out wrong—always does with me. That puts my idea of his giving me a rest on the bum.

MARTHY—What d'yuh mean?

ANNA—I s'pose he lives on the boat, don't he?

MARTHY—Sure. What about it? Can't you live on it, too?

ANNA—[Scornfully.] Me? On a dirty coal barge! What d'you think I am?

MARTHY—[Resentfully.] What d'yuh know about barges, huh? Bet yuh ain't never seen one. That's what comes of his bringing yuh up inland—away from the old devil sea—where yuh'd be safe—Gawd! [The irony of it strikes her sense of humor and she laughs hoarsely.]

ANNA—[Angrily.] His bringing me up! Is that what he tells people! I like his nerve! He let them cousins of my Old Woman's keep me on their farm and work me to death like a dog.

18

MARTHY—Well, he's got queer notions on some things. I've heard him say a farm was the best place for a kid.

ANNA—Sure. That's what he'd always answer back—and a lot of crazy stuff about staying away from the sea—stuff I couldn't make head or tail to. I thought he must be nutty.

MARTHY—He is on that one point. [Casually.] So yuh didn't fall for life on the farm, huh?

ANNA—I should say not! The old man of the family, his wife, and four sons—I had to slave for all of 'em. I was only a poor relation, and they treated me worse than they dare treat a hired girl. [After a moment's hesitation—somberly.] It was one of the sons—the youngest—started me—when I was sixteen. After that, I hated 'em so I'd killed 'em all if I'd stayed. So I run away—to St. Paul.

MARTHY—[Who has been listening sympathetically.] I've heard Old Chris talkin' about your bein' a nurse girl out there. Was that all a bluff yuh put up when yuh wrote him?

ANNA—Not on your life, it wasn't. It was true for two years. I didn't go wrong all at one jump. Being a nurse girl was yust what finished me. Taking care of other people's kids, always listening to their bawling and crying, caged in, when you're only a kid yourself and want to go out and see things. At last I got the chance—to get into that house. And you bet your life I took it! [Defiantly.] And I ain't sorry neither. [After a pause—with bitter hatred.] It was all men's fault—the whole business. It was men on the farm ordering and beating me—and giving me the wrong start. Then when I was a nurse, it was men again hanging around, bothering me, trying to see what they could get. [She gives a hard laugh.] And now it's men all the time. Gawd, I hate 'em all, every mother's son of 'em! Don't you?

MARTHY—Oh, I dunno. There's good ones and bad ones, kid. You've just had a run of bad luck with 'em, that's all. Your Old Man, now—old Chris—he's a good one.

19

ANNA—[Sceptically.] He'll have to show me.

MARTHY—Yuh kept right on writing him yuh was a nurse girl still, even after yuh was in the house, didn't yuh?

ANNA—Sure. [Cynically.] Not that I think he'd care a darn.

MARTHY—Yuh're all wrong about him, kid, [Earnestly.] I know Old Chris well for a long time. He's talked to me 'bout you lots o' times. He thinks the world o' you, honest he does.

ANNA—Aw, quit the kiddin'!

MARTHY—Honest! Only, he's a simple old guy, see? He's got nutty notions. But he means well, honest. Listen to me, kid—[She is interrupted by the opening and shutting of the street door in the bar and by hearing CHRIS' voice.] Ssshh!

ANNA—What's up?

CHRIS—[Who has entered the bar. He seems considerably sobered up.] Py golly, Larry, dat grub taste good. Marthy in back?

LARRY—Sure—and another tramp with her. [CHRIS starts for the entrance to the back room.]

MARTHY—[To ANNA in a hurried, nervous whisper.] That's him now. He's comin' in here. Brace up!

ANNA—Who? [Chris opens the door.]

MARTHY—[As if she were greeting him for the first time]. Why hello, Old Chris. [Then before he can speak, she shuffles hurriedly past him into the bar, beckoning him to follow her.] Come here. I wanta tell yuh somethin'. [He goes out to her. She speaks hurriedly in a low voice.] Listen! I'm goin' to beat it down to the barge—pack up me duds and blow. That's her in there—your Anna—just come—waitin' for yuh. Treat her right, see? She's been sick. Well, s'long! [She goes into the back room—to ANNA.] S'long, kid. I gotta beat it now. See yuh later.

20

ANNA—[Nervously.] So long. [MARTHY goes quickly out of the family entrance.] LARRY—[Looking at the stupefied CHRIS curiously.] Well, what's up now?

CHRIS—[Vaguely.] Nutting—nutting. [He stands before the door to the back room in an agony of embarrassed emotion—then he forces himself to a bold decision, pushes open the door and walks in. He stands there, casts a shy glance at ANNA, whose brilliant clothes, and, to him, high-toned appearance awe him terribly. He looks about him with pitiful nervousness as if to avoid the appraising look with which she takes in his face, his clothes, etc—his voice seeming to plead for her forbearance.] Anna!

ANNA—[Acutely embarrassed in her turn.] Hello—father. She told me it was you. I yust got here a little while ago.

CHRIS—[Goes slowly over to her chair.] It's good—for see you—after all dem years, Anna. [He bends down over her. After an embarrassed struggle they manage to kiss each other.]

ANNA—[A trace of genuine feeling in her voice.] It's good to see you, too.

CHRIS—[Grasps her arms and looks into her face—then overcome by a wave of fierce tenderness.] Anna lilla! Anna lilla! [Takes her in his arms.]

ANNA—[Shrinks away from him, half-frightened.] What's that—Swedish? I don't know it. [Then as if seeking relief from the tension in a voluble chatter.] Gee, I had an awful trip coming here. I'm all in. I had to sit up in the dirty coach all night—couldn't get no sleep, hardly—and then I had a hard job finding this place. I never been in New York before, you know, and—

CHRIS—[Who has been staring down at her face admiringly, not hearing what she says—impulsively.] You know you vas awful pooty gel, Anna? Ay bet all men see you fall in love with you, py yiminy!

21

ANNA—[Repelled—harshly.] Cut it! You talk same as they all do.

CHRIS—[Hurt—humbly.] Ain't no harm for your fader talk dat vay, Anna.

ANNA—[Forcing a short laugh.] No—course not. Only—it's funny to see you and not remember nothing. You're like—a stranger.

CHRIS—[Sadly.] Ay s'pose. Ay never come home only few times ven you vas kit in Sveden. You don't remember dat?

ANNA—No. [Resentfully.] But why didn't you never come home them days? Why didn't you never come out West to see me?

CHRIS—[Slowly.] Ay tank, after your mo'der die, ven Ay vas avay on voyage, it's better for you you don't never see me! [He sinks down in the chair opposite her dejectedly—then turns to her—sadly.] Ay don't know, Anna, vhy Ay never come home Sveden in ole year. Ay vant come home end of every voyage. Ay vant see your mo'der, your two bro'der before dey vas drowned, you ven you vas born—but—Ay—don't go. Ay sign on oder ships—go South America, go Australia, go China, go every port all over world many times—but Ay never go aboard ship sail for Sveden. Ven Ay gat money for pay passage home as passenger den—[He bows his head guiltily.] Ay forgat and Ay spend all money. Ven Ay tank again, it's too late. [He sighs.] Ay don't know vhy but dat's vay with most sailor fallar, Anna. Dat ole davil sea make dem crazy fools with her dirty tricks. It's so.

ANNA—[Who has watched him keenly while he has been speaking—with a trace of scorn in her voice.] Then you think the sea's to blame for everything, eh? Well, you're still workin' on it, ain't you, spite of all you used to write me about hating it. That dame was here told me you was captain of a coal barge—and you wrote me you was yanitor of a building!

CHRIS—[Embarrassed but lying glibly.] Oh, Ay work on land long time as yanitor. Yust short time ago Ay got dis yob cause Ay vas sick, need open air.

22

ANNA—[Sceptically.] Sick? You? You'd never think it.

CHRIS—And, Anna, dis ain't real sailor yob. Dis ain't real boat on sea. She's yust ole tub—like piece of land with house on it dat float. Yob on her ain't sea yob. No. Ay don't gat yob on sea, Anna, if Ay die first. Ay swear dat, ven your mo'der die. Ay keep my word, py yingo!

ANNA—[Perplexed.] Well, I can't see no difference. [Dismissing the subject.] Speaking of being sick, I been there myself—yust out of the hospital two weeks ago.

CHRIS—[Immediately all concern.] You, Anna? Py golly! [Anxiously.] You feel better now, dough, don't you? You look little tired, dat's all!

ANNA—[Wearily.] I am. Tired to death. I need a long rest and I don't see much chance of getting it.

CHRIS—What you mean, Anna?

ANNA—Well, when I made up my mind to come to see you, I thought you was a yanitor—that you'd have a place where, maybe, if you didn't mind having me, I could visit a while and rest up—till I felt able to get back on the job again.

CHRIS—[Eagerly.] But Ay gat place, Anna—nice place. You rest all you want, py yiminy! You don't never have to vork as nurse gel no more. You stay with me, py golly!

ANNA—[Surprised and pleased by his eagerness—with a smile.] Then you're really glad to see me—honest?

CHRIS—[Pressing one of her hands in both of his.] Anna, Ay like see you like hell, Ay tal you! And don't you talk no more about gatting yob. You stay with me. Ay don't see you for long time, you don't forgat dat. [His voice trembles.] Ay'm gatting ole. Ay gat no one in vorld but you.

ANNA—[Touched—embarrassed by this unfamiliar emotion.]

23

Thanks. It sounds good to hear someone—talk to me that way. Say, though—if you're so lonely—it's funny—why ain't you ever married again?

CHRIS—[Shaking his head emphatically—after a pause.] Ay love your mo'der too much for ever do dat, Anna.

ANNA—[Impressed—slowly.] I don't remember nothing about her. What was she like? Tell me.

CHRIS—Ay tal you all about everytang—and you tal me all tangs happen to you. But not here now. Dis ain't good place for young gel, anyway. Only no good sailor fallar come here for gat drunk. [He gets to his feet quickly and picks up her bag.] You come with me, Anna. You need lie down, gat rest.

ANNA—[Half rises to her feet, then sits down again.] Where're you going?

CHRIS—Come. Ve gat on board.

ANNA—[Disappointedly.] On board your barge, you mean? [Dryly.] Nix for mine! [Then seeing his crestfallen look—forcing a smile.] Do you think that's a good place for a young girl like me—a coal barge?

CHRIS—[Dully.] Yes, Ay tank. [He hesitates—then continues more and more pleadingly.] You don't know how nice it's on barge, Anna. Tug come and ve gat towed out on voyage—yust water all round, and sun, and fresh air, and good grub for make you strong, healthy gel. You see many tangs you don't see before. You gat moonlight at night, maybe; see steamer pass; see schooner make sail—see everytang dat's pooty. You need take rest like dat. You work too hard for young gel already. You need vacation, yes!

ANNA—[Who has listened to him with a growing interest—with an uncertain laugh.] It sounds good to hear you tell it. I'd sure like a trip on the water, all right. It's the barge idea has me stopped. Well, I'll go down with you and have a look—and maybe I'll take a chance. Gee, I'd do anything once.

24

CHRIS—[Picks up her bag again.] Ye go, eh?

ANNA—What's the rush? Wait a second. [Forgetting the situation for a moment, she relapses into the familiar form and flashes one of her winning trade smiles at him.] Gee, I'm thirsty.

CHRIS—[Sets down her bag immediately—hastily.] Ay'm sorry, Anna. What you tank you like for drink, eh?

ANNA—[Promptly.] I'll take a—[Then suddenly reminded—confusedly.] I don't know. What'a they got here?

CHRIS—[With a grin.] Ay don't tank dey got much fancy drink for young gel in dis place, Anna. Yinger ale—sas'prilla, maybe.

ANNA—[Forcing a laugh herself.] Make it sas, then.

CHRIS—[Coming up to her—with a wink.] Ay tal you, Anna, we calabrate, yes—dis one time because we meet after many year. [In a half whisper, embarrassedly.] Dey gat good port wine, Anna. It's good for you. Ay tank—little bit—for give you appetite. It ain't strong, neider. One glass don't go to your head, Ay promise.

ANNA—[With a half hysterical laugh.] All right! I'll take port.

CHRIS—Ay go gat him. [He goes out to the bar. As soon as the door closes, Anna starts to her feet.]

ANNA—[Picking up her bag—half—aloud—stammeringly.] Gawd, I can't stand this! I better beat it. [Then she lets her bag drop, stumbles over to her chair again, and covering her face with her hands, begins to sob.]

LARRY—[Putting down his paper as CHRIS comes up—with a grin.] Well, who's the blond?

CHRIS—[Proudly.] Dat vas Anna, Larry.

LARRY—[In amazement.] Your daughter, Anna? [CHRIS nods. LARRY lets a long, low whistle escape him and turns away embarrassedly.]

25

CHRIS—Don't you tank she vas pooty gel, Larry?

LARRY—[Rising to the occasion.] Sure! A peach!

CHRIS—You bet you! Give me drink for take back—one port vine for Anna—she calabrate dis one time with me—and small beer for me.

LARRY—[As he gets the drinks.] Small beer for you, eh? She's reformin' you already.

CHRIS—[Pleased.] You bet! [He takes the drinks. As she hears him coming, ANNA hastily dries her eyes, tries to smile. CHRIS comes in and sets the drinks down on the table—stares at her for a second anxiously—patting her hand.] You look tired, Anna. Veil, Ay make you take good long rest now. [Picking up his beer.] Come, you drink vine. It put new life in you. [She lifts her glass—he grins.] Skoal, Anna! You know dat Svedish word?

ANNA—Skoal! [Downing her port at a gulp like a drink of whiskey—her lips trembling.] Skoal? Guess I know that word, all right, all right!

[The Curtain Falls]

26

ACT II

SCENE—Ten days later. The stern of the deeply-laden barge, "SIMEON WINTHROP," at anchor in the outer harbor of Provincetown, Mass. It is ten o'clock at night. Dense fog shrouds the barge on all sides, and she floats motionless on a calm. A lantern set up on an immense coil of thick hawser sheds a dull, filtering light on objects near it—the heavy steel bits for making fast the tow lines, etc. In the rear is the cabin, its misty windows glowing wanly with the light of a lamp inside. The chimney of the cabin stove rises a few feet above the roof. The doleful tolling of bells, on Long Point, on ships at anchor, breaks the silence at regular intervals.

As the curtain rises, ANNA is discovered standing near the coil of rope on which the lantern is placed. She looks healthy, transformed, the natural color has come back to her face. She has on a black, oilskin coat, but wears no hat. She is staring out into the fog astern with an expression of awed wonder. The cabin door is pushed open and CHRIS appears. He is dressed in yellow oilskins—coat, pants, sou'wester—and wears high sea-boots.

CHRIS—[The glare from the cabin still in his eyes, peers blinkmgly astern.] Anna! [Receiving no reply, he calls again, this time with apparent apprehension.] Anna!

ANNA—[With a start—making a gesture with her hand as if to impose silence—in a hushed whisper.] Yes, here I am. What d'you want?

CHRIS—[Walks over to her—solicitously.] Don't you come turn in, Anna? It's late—after four bells. It ain't good for you stay out here in fog, Ay tank.

27

ANNA—Why not? [With a trace of strange exultation.] I love this fog! Honest! It's so—[She hesitates, groping for a word.]—Funny and still. I feel as if I was—out of things altogether.

CHRIS—[Spitting disgustedly.] Fog's vorst one of her dirty tricks, py yingo!

ANNA—[With a short laugh.] Beefing about the sea again? I'm getting so's I love it, the little I've seen.

CHRIS—[Glancing at her moodily.] Dat's foolish talk, Anna. You see her more, you don't talk dat vay. [Then seeing her irritation, he hastily adopts a more cheerful tone.] But Ay'm glad you like it on barge. Ay'm glad it makes you feel good again. [With a placating grin.] You like live like dis alone with ole fa'der, eh?

ANNA—Sure I do. Everything's been so different from anything I ever come across before. And now—this fog—Gee, I wouldn't have missed it for nothing. I never thought living on ships was so different from land. Gee, I'd just love to work on it, honest I would, if I was a man. I don't wonder you always been a sailor.

CHRIS—[Vehemently.] Ay ain't sailor, Anna. And dis ain't real sea. You only see nice part. [Then as she doesn't answer, he continues hopefully.] Vell, fog lift in morning, Ay tank.

ANNA—[The exultation again in her voice.] I love it! I don't give a rap if it never lifts! [CHRIS fidgets from one foot to the other worriedly. ANNA continues slowly, after a pause.] It makes me feel clean—out here—'s if I'd taken a bath.

CHRIS—[After a pause.] You better go in cabin—read book. Dat put you to sleep.

ANNA—I don't want to sleep. I want to stay out here—and think about things.

CHRIS—[Walks away from her toward the cabin—then comes back.] You act funny to-night, Anna.

28

ANNA—[Her voice rising angrily.] Say, what're you trying to do— make things rotten? You been kind as kind can be to me and I certainly appreciate it—only don't spoil it all now. [Then, seeing the hurt expression on her father's face, she forces a smile.] Let's talk of something else. Come. Sit down here. [She points to the coil of rope.]

CHRIS—[Sits down beside her with a sigh.] It's gatting pooty late in night, Anna. Must be near five bells.

ANNA—[Interestedly.] Five bells? What time is that?

CHRIS—Half past ten.

ANNA—Funny I don't know nothing about sea talk—but those cousins was always talking crops and that stuff. Gee, wasn't I sick of it—and of them!

CHRIS—You don't like live on farm, Anna?

ANNA—I've told you a hundred times I hated it. [Decidedly.] I'd rather have one drop of ocean than all the farms in the world! Honest! And you wouldn't like a farm, neither. Here's where you belong. [She makes a sweeping gesture seaward.] But not on a coal barge. You belong on a real ship, sailing all over the world.

CHRIS—[Moodily.] Ay've done dat many year, Anna, when Ay vas damn fool.

ANNA—[Disgustedly.] Oh, rats! [After a pause she speaks musingly.] Was the men in our family always sailors—as far back as you know about?

CHRIS—[Shortly.] Yes. Damn fools! All men in our village on coast, Sveden, go to sea. Ain't nutting else for dem to do. My fa'der die on board ship in Indian Ocean. He's buried at sea. Ay don't never know him only little bit. Den my tree bro'der, older'n me, dey go on ships. Den Ay go, too. Den my mo'der she's left all 'lone. She die pooty quick after dat—all 'lone. Ve vas all avay on voyage when she die. [He pauses sadly.] Two my bro'der dey gat lost on fishing

29

boat same like your bro'ders vas drowned. My oder bro'der, he save money, give up sea, den he die home in bed. He's only one dat ole davil don't kill. [Defiantly.] But me, Ay bet you Ay die ashore in bed, too!

ANNA—Were all of 'em yust plain sailors?

CHEIS—Able body seaman, most of dem. [With a certain pride.] Dey vas all smart seaman, too—A one. [Then after hesitating a moment—shyly.] Ay vas bo'sun.

ANNA—Bo'sun?

CHRIS—Dat's kind of officer.

ANNA—Gee, that was fine. What does he do?

CHRIS—[After a second's hesitation, plunged into gloom again by his fear of her enthusiasm.] Hard vork all time. It's rotten, Ay tal you, for go to sea. [Determined to disgust her with sea life— volubly.] Dey're all fool fallar, dem fallar in our family. Dey all vork rotten yob on sea for nutting, don't care nutting but yust gat big pay day in pocket, gat drunk, gat robbed, ship avay again on oder voyage. Dey don't come home, Dey don't do anytang like good man do. And dat ole davil, sea, sooner, later she svallow dem up.

ANNA—[With an excited laugh.] Good sports, I'd call 'em. [Then hastily.] But say—listen—did all the women of the family marry sailors?

CHRIS—[Eagerly—seeing a chance to drive home his point.] Yes— and it's bad on dem like hell vorst of all. Dey don't see deir men only once in long while. Dey set and vait all 'lone. And vhen deir boys grows up, go to sea, dey sit and vait some more. [Vehemently.] Any gel marry sailor, she's crazy fool! Your mo'der she tal you same tang if she vas alive. [He relapses into an attitude of somber brooding.]

ANNA—[After a pause—dreamily.] Funny! I do feel sort of—nutty, to-night. I feel old.

30

CHRIS—[Mystified.] Old?

ANNA—Sure—like I'd been living a long, long time—out here in the fog. [Frowning perplexedly.] I don't know how to tell you yust what I mean. It's like I'd come home after a long visit away some place. It all seems like I'd been here before lots of times—on boats— in this same fog. [With a short laugh.] You must think I'm off my base.

CHRIS—[Gruffly.] Anybody feel funny dat vay in fog.

ANNA—[Persistently.] But why d'you s'pose I feel so—so—like I'd found something I'd missed and been looking for—'s if this was the right place for me to fit in? And I seem to have forgot—everything that's happened—like it didn't matter no more. And I feel clean, somehow—like you feel yust after you've took a bath. And I feel happy for once—yes, honest!—happier than I ever been anywhere before! [As CHRIS makes no comment but a heavy sigh, she continues wonderingly.] It's nutty for me to feel that way, don't you think?

CHRIS—[A grim foreboding in his voice.] Ay tank Ay'm damn fool for bring you on voyage, Anna.

ANNA—[Impressed by his tone.] You talk—nutty to-night yourself. You act's if you was scared something was going to happen.

CHRIS—Only God know dat, Anna.

ANNA—[Half-mockingly.] Then it'll be Gawd's will, like the preachers say-what does happen.

CHRIS—[Starts to his feet with fierce protest.] No! Dat ole davil, sea, she ain't God! [In the pause of silence that comes after his defiance a hail in a man's husky, exhausted voice comes faintly out of the fog to port.] "Ahoy!" [CHRIS gives a startled exclamation.]

ANNA—[Jumping to her feet.] What's that?

31

CHRIS—[Who has regained his composure—sheepishly.] Py golly, dat scare me for minute. It's only some fallar hail, Anna—loose his course in fog. Must be fisherman's power boat. His engine break down, Ay guess. [The "ahoy" comes again through the wall of fog, sounding much nearer this time. CHRIS goes over to the port bulwark.] Sound from dis side. She come in from open sea. [He holds his hands to his mouth, megaphone-fashion, and shouts back.] Ahoy, dere! Vhat's trouble?

THE VOICE—[This time sounding nearer but up forward toward the bow.] Heave a rope when we come alongside. [Then irritably.] Where are ye, ye scut?

CHRIS—Ay hear dem rowing. Dey come up by bow, Ay tank. [Then shouting out again.] Dis vay!

THE VOICE—Right ye are! [There is a muffled sound of oars in oar-locks.]

ANNA—[Half to herself—resentfully.] Why don't that guy stay where he belongs?

CHRIS—[Hurriedly.] Ay go up bow. All hands asleep 'cepting fallar on vatch. Ay gat heave line to dat fallar. [He picks up a coil of rope and hurries off toward the bow. ANNA walks back toward the extreme stern as if she wanted to remain as much isolated possible. She turns her back on the proceedings and stares out into the fog. THE VOICE is heard again shouting "Ahoy" and CHRIS answering "Dis way" Then there is a pause—the murmur of excited voices— then the scuffling of feet. CHRIS appears from around the cabin to port. He is supporting the limp form of a man dressed in dungarees, holding one of the man's arms around his neck. The deckhand, JOHNSON, a young, blond Swede, follows him, helping along another exhausted man similar fashion. ANNA turns to look at them. Chris stops for a second—volubly.] Anna! You come help, vill you? You find vhiskey in cabin. Dese fallars need drink for fix dem. Dey vas near dead.

32

ANNA—[Hurrying to him.] Sure—but who are they? What's the trouble?

CHRIS—Sailor fallars. Deir steamer gat wrecked. Dey been five days in open boat—four fallars—only one left able stand up. Come, Anna. [She precedes him into the cabin, holding the door open while he and JOHNSON carry in their burdens. The door is shut, then opened again as JOHNSON comes out. CHRIS'S voice shouts after him.] Go gat oder fallar, Yohnson.

JOHNSON—Yes, sir. [He goes. The door is closed again. MAT BURKE stumbles in around the port side of the cabin. He moves slowly, feeling his way uncertainly, keeping hold of the port bulwark with his right hand to steady himself. He is stripped to the waist, has on nothing but a pair of dirty dungaree pants. He is a powerful, broad-chested six-footer, his face handsome in a hard, rough, bold, defiant way. He is about thirty, in the full power of his heavy-muscled, immense strength. His dark eyes are bloodshot and wild from sleeplessness. The muscles of his arms and shoulders are lumped in knots and bunches, the veins of his forearms stand out like blue cords. He finds his way to the coil of hawser and sits down on it facing the cabin, his back bowed, head in his hands, in an attitude of spent weariness.]

BURKE—[Talking aloud to himself.] Row, ye divil! Row! [Then lifting his head and looking about him.] What's this tub? Well, we're safe anyway—with the help of God. [He makes the sign of the cross mechanically. JOHNSON comes along the deck to port, supporting the fourth man, who is babbling to himself incoherently. BURKE glances at him disdainfully.] Is it losing the small wits ye iver had, ye are? Deck-scrubbing scut! [They pass him and go into the cabin, leaving the door open. BURKE sags forward wearily.] I'm bate out—bate out entirely.

ANNA—[Comes out of the cabin with a tumbler quarter-full of whiskey in her hand. She gives a start when she sees BURKE so near her, the light from the open door falling full on him. Then, overcoming what is evidently a feeling of repulsion, she comes up

33

beside him.] Here you are. Here's a drink for you. You need it, I guess.

BURKE—[Lifting his head slowly—confusedly.] Is it dreaming I am?

ANNA—[Half smiling.] Drink it and you'll find it ain't no dream.

BURKE—To hell with the drink—but I'll take it just the same. [He tosses it down.] Aah! I'm needin' that—and 'tis fine stuff. [Looking up at her with frank, grinning admiration.] But 'twasn't the booze I meant when I said, was I dreaming. I thought you was some mermaid out of the sea come to torment me. [He reaches out to feel of her arm.] Aye, rale flesh and blood, divil a less.

ANNA—[Coldly. Stepping back from him.] Cut that.

BURKE—But tell me, isn't this a barge I'm on—or isn't it?

ANNA—Sure.

BURKE—And what is a fine handsome woman the like of you doing on this scow?

ANNA—[Coldly.] Never you mind. [Then half-amused in spite of herself.] Say, you're a great one, honest—starting right in kidding after what you been through.

BURKE—[Delighted—proudly.] Ah, it was nothing—aisy for a rale man with guts to him, the like of me. [He laughs.] All in the day's work, darlin'. [Then, more seriously but still in a boastful tone, confidentially.] But I won't be denying 'twas a damn narrow squeak. We'd all ought to be with Davy Jones at the bottom of the sea, be rights. And only for me, I'm telling you, and the great strength and guts is in me, we'd be being scoffed by the fishes this minute!

ANNA—[Contemptuously.] Gee, you hate yourself, don't you? [Then turning away from him indifferently.] Well, you'd better come in and lie down. You must want to sleep.

34

BURKE—[Stung—rising unsteadily to his feet with chest out and head thrown back—resentfully.] Lie down and sleep, is it? Divil a wink I'm after having for two days and nights and divil a bit I'm needing now. Let you not be thinking I'm the like of them three weak scuts come in the boat with me. I could lick the three of them sitting down with one hand tied behind me. They may be bate out, but I'm not—and I've been rowing the boat with them lying in the bottom not able to raise a hand for the last two days we was in it. [Furiously, as he sees this is making no impression on her.] And I can lick all hands on this tub, wan be wan, tired as I am!

ANNA—[Sarcastically.] Gee, ain't you a hard guy! [Then, with a trace of sympathy, as she notices him swaying from weakness.] But never mind that fight talk. I'll take your word for all you've said. Go on and sit down out here, anyway, if I can't get you to come inside. [He sits down weakly.] You're all in, you might as well own up to it.

BURKE—[Fiercely.] The hell I am!

ANNA—[Coldly.] Well, be stubborn then for all I care. And I must say I don't care for your language. The men I know don't pull that rough stuff when ladies are around.

BURKE—[Getting unsteadily to his feet again—in a rage.] Ladies! Ho-ho! Divil mend you! Let you not be making game of me. What would ladies be doing on this bloody hulk? [As ANNA attempts to go to the cabin, he lurches into her path.] Aisy, now! You're not the old Square-head's woman, I suppose you'll be telling me next—living in his cabin with him, no less! [Seeing the cold, hostile expression on ANNA's face, he suddenly changes his tone to one of boisterous joviality.] But I do be thinking, iver since the first look my eyes took at you, that it's a fool you are to be wasting yourself—a fine, handsome girl—on a stumpy runt of a man like that old Swede. There's too many strapping great lads on the sea would give their heart's blood for one kiss of you!

ANNA—[Scornfully.] Lads like you, eh?

35

BURKE—[Grinning.] Ye take the words out o' my mouth. I'm the proper lad for you, if it's meself do be saying it. [With a quick movement he puts his arms about her waist.] Whisht, now, me daisy! Himself's in the cabin. It's wan of your kisses I'm needing to take the tiredness from me bones. Wan kiss, now! [He presses her to him and attempts to kiss her.]

ANNA—[Struggling fiercely.] Leggo of me, you big mut! [She pushes him away with all her might. BURKE, weak and tottering, is caught off his guard. He is thrown down backward and, in falling, hits his head a hard thump against the bulwark. He lies there still, knocked out for the moment. ANNA stands for a second, looking down at him frightenedly. Then she kneels down beside him and raises his head to her knee, staring into his face anxiously for some sign of life.]

BURKE—[Stirring a bit—mutteringly.] God stiffen it! [He opens his eyes and blinks up at her with vague wonder.]

ANNA—[Letting his head sink back on the deck, rising to her feet with a sigh of relief.] You're coming to all right, eh? Gee, I was scared for a moment I'd killed you.

BURKE—[With difficulty rising to a sitting position—scornfully.] Killed, is it? It'd take more than a bit of a blow to crack my thick skull. [Then looking at her with the most intense admiration.] But, glory be, it's a power of strength is in them two fine arms of yours. There's not a man in the world can say the same as you, that he seen Mat Burke lying at his feet and him dead to the world.

ANNA—[Rather remorsefully.] Forget it. I'm sorry it happened, see? [BURKE rises and sits on bench. Then severely.] Only you had no right to be getting fresh with me. Listen, now, and don't go getting any more wrong notions. I'm on this barge because I'm making a trip with my father. The captain's my father. Now you know.

BURKE—The old square—the old Swede, I mean?

36

ANNA—Yes.

BURKE—[Rising—peering at her face.] Sure I might have known it, if I wasn't a bloody fool from birth. Where else'd you get that fine yellow hair is like a golden crown on your head.

ANNA—[With an amused laugh.] Say, nothing stops you, does it? [Then attempting a severe tone again.] But don't you think you ought to be apologizing for what you said and done yust a minute ago, instead of trying to kid me with that mush?

BURKE—[Indignantly.] Mush! [Then bending forward toward her with very intense earnestness.] Indade and I will ask your pardon a thousand times—and on my knees, if ye like. I didn't mean a word of what I said or did. [Resentful again for a second.] But divil a woman in all the ports of the world has iver made a great fool of me that way before!

ANNA—[With amused sarcasm.] I see. You mean you're a lady-killer and they all fall for you.

BURKE—[Offended. Passionately.] Leave off your fooling! 'Tis that is after getting my back up at you. [Earnestly.] 'Tis no lie I'm telling you about the women. [Ruefully.] Though it's a great jackass I am to be mistaking you, even in anger, for the like of them cows on the waterfront is the only women I've met up with since I was growed to a man. [As ANNA shrinks away from him at this, he hurries on pleadingly.] I'm a hard, rough man and I'm not fit, I'm thinking, to be kissing the shoe-soles of a fine, dacent girl the like of yourself. 'Tis only the ignorance of your kind made me see you wrong. So you'll forgive me, for the love of God, and let us be friends from this out. [Passionately.] I'm thinking I'd rather be friends with you than have my wish for anything else in the world. [He holds out his hand to her shyly.]

ANNA—[Looking queerly at him, perplexed and worried, but moved and pleased in spite of herself—takes his hand uncertainly.] Sure.

37

BURKE—[With boyish delight.] God bless you! [In his excitement he squeezes her hand tight.]

ANNA—Ouch!

BURKE—[Hastily dropping her hand—ruefully.] Your pardon, Miss. 'Tis a clumsy ape I am. [Then simply—glancing down his arm proudly.] It's great power I have in my hand and arm, and I do be forgetting it at times.

ANNA—[Nursing her crushed hand and glancing at his arm, not without a trace of his own admiration.] Gee, you're some strong, all right.

BURKE—[Delighted.] It's no lie, and why shouldn't I be, with me shoveling a million tons of coal in the stokeholes of ships since I was a lad only. [He pats the coil of hawser invitingly.] Let you sit down, now, Miss, and I'll be telling you a bit of myself, and you'll be telling me a bit of yourself, and in an hour we'll be as old friends as if we was born in the same house. [He pulls at her sleeve shyly.] Sit down now, if you plaze.

ANNA—[With a half laugh.] Well—[She sits down.] But we won't talk about me, see? You tell me about yourself and about the wreck.

BURKE—[Flattered.] I'll tell you, surely. But can I be asking you one question. Miss, has my head in a puzzle?

ANNA—[Guardedly.] Well—I dunno—what is it?

BURKE—What is it you do when you're not taking a trip with the Old Man? For I'm thinking a fine girl the like of you ain't living always on this tub.

ANNA—[Uneasily.] No—of course I ain't. [She searches his face suspiciously, afraid there may be some hidden insinuation in his words. Seeing his simple frankness, she goes on confidently.] Well, I'll tell you. I'm a governess, see? I take care of kids for people and learn them things.

BURKE—[Impressed.] A governess, is it? You must be smart, surely.

ANNA—But let's not talk about me. Tell me about the wreck, like you promised me you would.

BURKE—[Importantly.] 'Twas this way, Miss. Two weeks out we ran into the divil's own storm, and she sprang wan hell of a leak up for'ard. The skipper was hoping to make Boston before another blow would finish her, but ten days back we met up with another storm the like of the first, only worse. Four days we was in it with green seas raking over her from bow to stern. That was a terrible time, God help us. [Proudly.] And if 'twasn't for me and my great strength, I'm telling you—and it's God's truth—there'd been mutiny itself in the stokehole. 'Twas me held them to it, with a kick to wan and a clout to another, and they not caring a damn for the engineers any more, but fearing a clout of my right arm more than they'd fear the sea itself. [He glances at her anxiously, eager for her approval.]

ANNA—[Concealing a smile—amused by this boyish boasting of his.] You did some hard work, didn't you?

BURKE—[Promptly.] I did that! I'm a divil for sticking it out when them that's weak give up. But much good it did anyone! 'Twas a mad, fightin' scramble in the last seconds with each man for himself. I disremember how it come about, but there was the four of us in wan boat and when we was raised high on a great wave I took a look about and divil a sight there was of ship or men on top of the sea.

ANNA—[In a subdued voice.] Then all the others was drowned?

BURKE—They was, surely.

ANNA—[With a shudder.] What a terrible end!

BURKE—[Turns to her.] A terrible end for the like of them swabs does live on land, maybe. But for the like of us does be roaming the seas, a good end, I'm telling you—quick and clane.

ANNA—[Struck by the word.] Yes, clean. That's yust the word for—all of it—the way it makes me feel.

BURKE—The sea, you mean? [Interestedly.] I'm thinking you have a bit of it in your blood, too. Your Old Man wasn't only a barge rat—begging your pardon—all his life, by the cut of him.

ANNA—No, he was bo'sun on sailing ships for years. And all the men on both sides of the family have gone to sea as far back as he remembers, he says. All the women have married sailors, too.

BURKE—[With intense satisfaction.] Did they, now? They had spirit in them. It's only on the sea you'd find rale men with guts is fit to wed with fine, high-tempered girls [Then he adds half-boldly] the like of yourself.

ANNA—[With a laugh.] There you go kiddin' again. [Then seeing his hurt expression—quickly.] But you was going to tell me about yourself. You're Irish, of course I can tell that.

BURKE—[Stoutly.] Yes, thank God, though I've not seen a sight of it in fifteen years or more.

ANNA—[Thoughtfully.] Sailors never do go home hardly, do they? That's what my father was saying.

BURKE—He wasn't telling no lie. [With sudden melancholy.] It's a hard and lonesome life, the sea is. The only women you'd meet in the ports of the world who'd be willing to speak you a kind word isn't woman at all. You know the kind I mane, and they're a poor, wicked lot, God forgive them. They're looking to steal the money from you only.

ANNA—[Her face averted—rising to her feet—agitatedly.] I think—I guess I'd better see what's doing inside.

BURKE—[Afraid he has offended her—beseechingly.] Don't go, I'm saying! Is it I've given you offence with my talk of the like of them? Don't heed it at all! I'm clumsy in my wits when it comes to talking proper with a girl the like of you. And why wouldn't I be? Since the day I left home for to go to sea punching coal, this is the first time I've had a word with a rale, dacent woman. So don't turn your back on me now, and we beginning to be friends.

ANNA—[Turning to him again—forcing a smile.] I'm not sore at you, honest.

BURKE—[Gratefully.] God bless you!

ANNA—[Changing the subject abruptly.] But if you honestly think the sea's such a rotten life, why don't you get out of it?

BURKE—[Surprised.] Work on land, is it? [She nods. He spits scornfully.] Digging spuds in the muck from dawn to dark, I suppose? [Vehemently.] I wasn't made for it, Miss.

ANNA—[With a laugh.] I thought you'd say that.

BURKE—[Argumentatively.] But there's good jobs and bad jobs at sea, like there'd be on land. I'm thinking if it's in the stokehole of a proper liner I was, I'd be able to have a little house and be home to it wan week out of four. And I'm thinking that maybe then I'd have the luck to find a fine dacent girl—the like of yourself, now—would be willing to wed with me.

ANNA—[Turning away from him with a short laugh—uneasily.] Why, sure. Why not?

BURKE—[Edging up close to her—exultantly.] Then you think a girl the like of yourself might maybe not mind the past at all but only be seeing the good herself put in me?

ANNA—[In the same tone.] Why, sure.

BURKE—[Passionately.] She'd not be sorry for it, I'd take my oath! 'Tis no more drinking and roving about I'd be doing then, but giving my pay day into her hand and staying at home with her as meek as a lamb each night of the week I'd be in port.

ANNA—[Moved in spite of herself and troubled by this half-

41

concealed proposal—with a forced laugh.] All you got to do is find the girl.

BURKE—I have found her!

ANNA—[Half-frightenedly—trying to laugh it off.] You have? When? I thought you was saying—

BURKE—[Boldly and forcefully.] This night. [Hanging his head—humbly.] If she'll be having me. [Then raising his eyes to hers—simply.] 'Tis you I mean.

ANNA—[Is held by his eyes for a moment—then shrinks back from him with a strange, broken laugh.] Say—are you—going crazy? Are you trying to kid me? Proposing—to me!—for Gawd's sake!—on such short acquaintance? [CHRIS comes out of the cabin and stands staring blinkingly astern. When he makes out ANNA in such intimate proximity to this strange sailor, an angry expression comes over his face.]

BURKE—[Following her—with fierce, pleading insistence.] I'm telling you there's the will of God in it that brought me safe through the storm and fog to the wan spot in the world where you was! Think of that now, and isn't it queer—

CHRIS—Anna! [He comes toward them, raging, his fists clenched.] Anna, you gat in cabin, you hear!

ANNA—[All her emotions immediately transformed into resentment at his bullying tone.] Who d'you think you're talking to—a slave?

CHRIS—[Hurt—his voice breaking—pleadingly.] You need gat rest, Anna. You gat sleep. [She does not move. He turns on BURKE furiously.] What you doing here, you sailor fallar? You ain't sick like oders. You gat in fo'c's'tle. Dey give you bunk. [Threateningly.] You hurry, Ay tal you!

ANNA—[Impulsively.] But he is sick. Look at him. He can hardly stand up.

42

BURKE—[Straightening and throwing out his chest—with a bold laugh.] Is it giving me orders ye are, me bucko? Let you look out, then! With wan hand, weak as I am, I can break ye in two and fling the pieces over the side—and your crew after you. [Stopping abruptly.] I was forgetting. You're her Old Man and I'd not raise a fist to you for the world. [His knees sag, he wavers and seems about to fall. ANNA utters an exclamation of alarm and hurries to his slde.]

ANNA—[Taking one of his arms over her shoulder.] Come on in the cabin. You can have my bed if there ain't no other place.

BURKE—[With jubilant happiness—as they proceed toward the cabin.] Glory be to God, is it holding my arm about your neck you are! Anna! Anna! Sure it's a sweet name is suited to you.

ANNA—[Guiding him carefully.] Sssh! Sssh!

BURKE—Whisht, is it? Indade, and I'll not. I'll be roaring it out like a fog horn over the sea! You're the girl of the world and we'll be marrying soon and I don't care who knows it!

ANNA—[As she guides him through the cabin door.] Ssshh! Never mind that talk. You go to sleep. [They go out of sight in the cabin. CHRIS, who has been listening to BURKE's last words with open-mouthed amazement stands looking after them helplessly.]

CHRIS—[Turns suddenly and shakes his fist out at the sea—with bitter hatred.] Dat's your dirty trick, damn ole davil, you! [Then in a frenzy of rage.] But, py God, you don't do dat! Not while Ay'm living! No, py God, you don't!

[The Curtain Falls]

43

ACT III

SCENE—The interior of the cabin on the barge, "Simeon Winthrop" (at dock in Boston)—a narrow, low-ceilinged compartment the walls of which are painted a light brown with white trimmings. In the rear on the left, a door leading to the sleeping quarters. In the far left corner, a large locker-closet, painted white, on the door of which a mirror hangs on a nail. In the rear wall, two small square windows and a door opening out on the deck toward the stern. In the right wall, two more windows looking out on the port deck. White curtains, clean and stiff, are at the windows. A table with two cane-bottomed chairs stands in the center of the cabin. A dilapidated, wicker rocker, painted brown, is also by the table.

It is afternoon of a sunny day about a week later. From the harbor and docks outside, muffled by the closed door and windows, comes the sound of steamers' whistles and the puffing snort of the donkey engines of some ship unloading nearby.

As the curtain rises, CHRIS and ANNA are discovered. ANNA is seated in the rocking-chair by the table, with a newspaper in her hands. She is not reading but staring straight in front of her. She looks unhappy, troubled, frowningly concentrated on her thoughts. CHRIS wanders about the room, casting quick, uneasy side glances at her face, then stopping to peer absentmindedly out of the window. His attitude betrays an overwhelming, gloomy anxiety which has him on tenter hooks. He pretends to be engaged in setting things ship-shape, but this occupation is confined to picking up some object, staring at it stupidly for a second, then aimlessly putting it down again. He clears his throat and starts to sing to himself in a low, doleful voice: "My Yosephine, come aboard de ship. Long time Ay wait for you."

44

ANNA—[Turning on him, sarcastically.] I'm glad someone's feeling good. [Wearily.] Gee, I sure wish we was out of this dump and back in New York.

CHRIS—[With a sigh.] Ay'm glad vhen ve sail again, too. [Then, as she makes no comment, he goes on with a ponderous attempt at sarcasm.] Ay don't see vhy you don't like Boston, dough. You have good time here, Ay tank. You go ashore all time, every day and night veek ve've been here. You go to movies, see show, gat all kinds fun—[His eyes hard with hatred.] All with that damn Irish fallar!

ANNA—[With weary scorn.] Oh, for heaven's sake, are you off on that again? Where's the harm in his taking me around? D'you want me to sit all day and night in this cabin with you—and knit? Ain't I got a right to have as good a time as I can?

CHRIS—It ain't right kind of fun—not with that fallar, no.

ANNA—I been back on board every night by eleven, ain't I? [Then struck by some thought—looks at him with keen suspicion—with rising anger.] Say, look here, what d'you mean by what you yust said?

CHRIS—[Hastily.] Nutting but what Ay say, Anna.

ANNA—You said "ain't right" and you said it funny. Say, listen here, you ain't trying to insinuate that there's something wrong between us, are you?

CHRIS—[Horrified.] No, Anna! No, Ay svear to God, Ay never tank dat!

ANNA—[Mollified by his very evident sincerity—sitting down again.] Well, don't you never think it neither if you want me ever to speak to you again. [Angrily again.] If I ever dreamt you thought that, I'd get the hell out of this barge so quick you couldn't see me for dust.

CHRIS—[Soothingly.] Ay wouldn't never dream—[Then, after a

45

second's pause, reprovingly.] You vas gatting learn to svear. Dat ain't nice for young gel, you tank?

ANNA—[With a faint trace of a smile.] Excuse me. You ain't used to such language, I know. [Mockingly.] That's what your taking me to sea has done for me.

CHRIS—[Indignantly.] No, it ain't me. It's dat damn sailor fallar learn you bad tangs.

ANNA—He ain't a sailor. He's a stoker.

CHRIS—[Forcibly.] Dat vas million times vorse, Ay tal you! Dem fallars dat vork below shoveling coal vas de dirtiest, rough gang of no-good fallars in vorld!

ANNA—I'd hate to hear you say that to Mat.

CHRIS—Oh, Ay tal him same tang. You don't gat it in head Ay'm scared of him yust 'cause he vas stronger'n Ay vas. [Menacingly.] You don't gat for fight with fists with dem fallars. Dere's oder vay for fix him.

ANNA—[Glancing at him with sudden alarm.] What d'you mean?

CHRIS—[Sullenly.] Nutting.

ANNA—You'd better not. I wouldn't start no trouble with him if I was you. He might forget some time that you was old and my father—and then you'd be out of luck.

CHRIS—[With smouldering hatred.] Vell, yust let him! Ay'm ole bird maybe, but Ay bet Ay show him trick or two.

ANNA—[Suddenly changing her tone—persuasively.] Aw come on, be good. What's eating you, anyway? Don't you want no one to be nice to me except yourself?

CHRIS—[Placated—coming to her—eagerly.] Yes, Ay do, Anna— only not fallar on sea. But Ay like for you marry steady fallar got good yob on land. You have little home in country all your own—

46

ANNA—[Rising to her feet—brusquely.] Oh, cut it out! [Scornfully.] Little home in the country! I wish you could have seen the little home in the country where you had me in jail till I was sixteen! [With rising irritation.] Some day you're going to get me so mad with that talk, I'm going to turn loose on you and tell you—a lot of things that'll open your eyes.

CHRIS—[Alarmed.] Ay don't vant—

ANNA—I know you don't; but you keep on talking yust the same.

CHRIS—Ay don't talk no more den, Anna.

ANNA—Then promise me you'll cut out saying nasty things about Mat Burke every chance you get.

CHRIS—[Evasive and suspicious.] Vhy? You like dat fallar—very much, Anna?

ANNA—Yes, I certainly do! He's a regular man, no matter what faults he's got. One of his fingers is worth all the hundreds of men I met out there—inland.

CHRIS—[His face darkening.] Maybe you tank you love him, den?

ANNA—[Defiantly.] What of it if I do?

CHRIS—[Scowling and forcing out the words.] Maybe—you tank you—marry him?

ANNA—[Shaking her head.] No! [CHRIS' face lights up with relief. ANNA continues slowly, a trace of sadness in her voice.] If I'd met him four years ago—or even two years ago—I'd have jumped at the chance, I tell you that straight. And I would now—only he's such a simple guy—a big kid—and I ain't got the heart to fool him. [She breaks off suddenly.] But don't never say again he ain't good enough for me. It's me ain't good enough for him.

CHRIS—[Snorts scornfully.] Py yiminy, you go crazy, Ay tank!

ANNA—[With a mournful laugh.] Well, I been thinking I was
47

myself the last few days. [She goes and takes a shawl from a hook near the door and throws it over her shoulders.] Guess I'll take a walk down to the end of the dock for a minute and see what's doing. I love to watch the ships passing. Mat'll be along before long, I guess. Tell him where I am, will you?

CHRIS—[Despondently.] All right, Ay tal him. [ANNA goes out the doorway on rear. CHRIS follows her out and stands on the deck outside for a moment looking after her. Then he comes back inside and shuts the door. He stands looking out of the window— mutters—"Dirty die davil, you." Then he goes to the table, sets the cloth straight mechanically, picks up the newspaper ANNA has let fall to the floor and sits down in the rocking-chair. He stares at the paper for a while, then puts it on table, holds his head in his hands and sighs drearily. The noise of a man's heavy footsteps comes from the deck outside and there is a loud knock on the door. CHRIS starts, makes a move as if to get up and go to the door, then thinks better of it and sits still. The knock is repeated—then as no answer comes, the door is flung open and MAT BURKE appears. CHRIS scowls at the intruder and his hand instinctively goes back to the sheath knife on his hip. BURKE is dressed up—wears a cheap blue suit, a striped cotton shirt with a black tie, and black shoes newly shined. His face is beaming with good humor.]

BURKE—[As he sees CHRIS—in a jovial tone of mockery.] Well, God bless who's here! [He bends down and squeezes his huge form through the narrow doorway.] And how is the world treating you this afternoon, Anna's father?

CHRIS—[Sullenly.] Pooty goot—if it ain't for some fallars. BURKE—[With a grin.] Meaning me, do you? [He laughs.] Well, if you ain't the funny old crank of a man! [Then soberly.] Where's herself? [CHRIS sits dumb, scowling, his eyes averted. BURKE is irritated by this silence.] Where's Anna, I'm after asking you?

CHRIS—[Hesitating—then grouchily.] She go down end of dock.

BURKE—I'll be going down to her, then. But first I'm thinking I'll take this chance when we're alone to have a word with you. [He sits down opposite CHRIS at the table and leans over toward him.] And that word is soon said. I'm marrying your Anna before this day is out, and you might as well make up your mind to it whether you like it or no.

CHRIS—[Glaring at him with hatred and forcing a scornful laugh.] Ho-ho! Dat's easy for say!

BURKE—You mean I won't? [Scornfully.] Is it the like of yourself will stop me, are you thinking?

CHRIS—Yes, Ay stop it, if it come to vorst.

BURKE—[With scornful pity.] God help you!

CHRIS—But ain't no need for me do dat. Anna—

BURKE—[Smiling confidently.] Is it Anna you think will prevent me?

CHRIS—Yes.

BURKE—And I'm telling you she'll not. She knows I'm loving her, and she loves me the same, and I know it.

CHRIS—Ho-ho! She only have fun. She make big fool of you, dat's all!

BURKE—[Unshaken—pleasantly.] That's a lie in your throat, divil mend you!

CHRIS—No, it ain't lie. She tal me yust before she go out she never marry fallar like you.

BURKE—I'll not believe it. 'Tis a great old liar you are, and a divil to be making a power of trouble if you had your way. But 'tis not trouble I'm looking for, and me sitting down here. [Earnestly.] Let us be talking it out now as man to man. You're her father, and wouldn't it be a shame for us to be at each other's throats like a pair

49

of dogs, and I married with Anna. So out with the truth, man alive. What is it you're holding against me at all?

CHRIS—[A bit placated, in spite of himself, by BURKE'S evident sincerity—but puzzled and suspicious.] Vell—Ay don't vant for Anna gat married. Listen, you fallar. Ay'm a ole man. Ay don't see Anna for fifteen year. She vas all Ay gat in vorld. And now ven she come on first trip—you tank Ay vant her leave me 'lone again?

BURKE—[Heartily.] Let you not be thinking I have no heart at all for the way you'd be feeling.

CHRIS—[Astonished and encouraged—trying to plead persuasively.] Den you do right tang, eh? You ship avay again, leave Anna alone. [Cajolingly.] Big fallar like you dat's on sea, he don't need vife. He gat new gel in every port, you know dat.

BURKE—[Angry for a second.] God stiffen you! [Then controlling himself—calmly.] I'll not be giving you the lie on that. But divil take you, there's a time comes to every man, on sea or land, that isn't a born fool, when he's sick of the lot of them cows, and wearing his heart out to meet up with a fine dacent girl, and have a home to call his own and be rearing up children in it. 'Tis small use you're asking me to leave Anna. She's the wan woman of the world for me, and I can't live without her now, I'm thinking.

CHRIS—You forgat all about her in one veek out of port, Ay bet you!

BURKE—You don't know the like I am. Death itself wouldn't make me forget her. So let you not be making talk to me about leaving her. I'll not, and be damned to you! It won't be so bad for you as you'd make out at all. She'll be living here in the States, and her married to me. And you'd be seeing her often so—a sight more often than ever you saw her the fifteen years she was growing up in the West. It's quare you'd be the one to be making great trouble about her leaving you when you never laid eyes on her once in all them years.

CHRIS—[Guiltily.] Ay taught it vas better Anna stay avay, grow up inland where she don't ever know ole davil, sea.

BURKE—[Scornfully.] Is it blaming the sea for your troubles ye are again, God help you? Well, Anna knows it now. 'Twas in her blood, anyway.

CHRIS—And Ay don't vant she ever know no-good fallar on sea—

BURKE—She knows one now.

CHRIS—[Banging the table with his fist—furiously.] Dat's yust it! Dat's yust what you are—no-good, sailor fallar! You tank Ay lat her life be made sorry by you like her mo'der's vas by me! No, Ay svear! She don't marry you if Ay gat kill you first!

BURKE—[Looks at him a moment, in astonishment—then laughing uproariously.] Ho-ho! Glory be to God, it's bold talk you have for a stumpy runt of a man!

CHRIS—[Threateningly.] Vell—you see!

BURKE—[With grinning defiance.] I'll see, surely! I'll see myself and Anna married this day, I'm telling you! [Then with contemptuous exasperation.] It's quare fool's blather you have about the sea done this and the sea done that. You'd ought to be shamed to be saying the like, and you an old sailor yourself. I'm after hearing a lot of it from you and a lot more that Anna's told me you do be saying to her, and I'm thinking it's a poor weak thing you are, and not a man at all!

CHRIS—[Darkly.] You see if Ay'm man—maybe quicker'n you tank.

BURKE—[Contemptuously.] Yerra, don't be boasting. I'm thinking 'tis out of your wits you've got with fright of the sea. You'd be wishing Anna married to a farmer, she told me. That'd be a swate match, surely! Would you have a fine girl the like of Anna lying down at nights with a muddy scut stinking of pigs and dung? Or

51

would you have her tied for life to the like of them skinny, shrivelled swabs does be working in cities?

CHRIS—Dat's lie, you fool!

BURKE—'Tis not. 'Tis your own mad notions I'm after telling. But you know the truth in your heart, if great fear of the sea has made you a liar and coward itself. [Pounding the table.] The sea's the only life for a man with guts in him isn't afraid of his own shadow! 'Tis only on the sea he's free, and him roving the face of the world, seeing all things, and not giving a damn for saving up money, or stealing from his friends, or any of the black tricks that a landlubber'd waste his life on. 'Twas yourself knew it once, and you a bo'sun for years.

CHRIS—[Sputtering with rage.] You vas crazy fool, Ay tal you!

BURKE—You've swallowed the anchor. The sea give you a clout once knocked you down, and you're not man enough to get up for another, but lie there for the rest of your life howling bloody murder. [Proudly.] Isn't it myself the sea has nearly drowned, and me battered and bate till I was that close to hell I could hear the flames roaring, and never a groan out of me till the sea gave up and it seeing the great strength and guts of a man was in me?

CHRIS—[Scornfully.] Yes, you vas hell of fallar, hear you tal it!

BURKE—[Angrily.] You'll be calling me a liar once too often, me old bucko! Wasn't the whole story of it and my picture itself in the newspapers of Boston a week back? [Looking CHRIS up and down belittlingly.] Sure I'd like to see you in the best of your youth do the like of what I done in the storm and after. 'Tis a mad lunatic, screeching with fear, you'd be this minute!

CHRIS—Ho-ho! You vas young fool! In ole years when Ay was on windyammer, Ay vas through hundred storms vorse'n dat! Ships vas ships den—and men dat sail on dem vas real men. And now what you gat on steamers? You gat fallars on deck don't know ship from mudscow. [With a meaning glance at BURKE.] And below

52

deck you gat fallars yust know how for shovel coal—might yust as veil vork on coal vagon ashore!

BURKE—[Stung—angrily.] Is it casting insults at the men in the stokehole ye are, ye old ape? God stiffen you! Wan of them is worth any ten stock-fish-swilling Square-heads ever shipped on a windbag!

CHRIS—[His face working with rage, his hand going back to the sheath-knife on his hip.] Irish svine, you!

BURKE—[Tauntingly.] Don't ye like the Irish, ye old babboon? 'Tis that you're needing in your family, I'm telling you—an Irishman and a man of the stokehole—to put guts in it so that you'll not be having grandchildren would be fearful cowards and jackasses the like of yourself!

CHRIS—[Half rising from his chair—in a voice choked with rage.] You look out!

BURKE—[Watching him intently—a mocking smile on his lips.] And it's that you'll be having, no matter what you'll do to prevent; for Anna and me'll be married this day, and no old fool the like of you will stop us when I've made up my mind.

CHRIS—[With a hoarse cry.] You don't! [He throws himself at BURKE, knife in hand, knocking his chair over backwards. BURKE springs to his feet quickly in time to meet the attack. He laughs with the pure love of battle. The old Swede is like a child in his hands. BURKE does not strike or mistreat him in any way, but simply twists his right hand behind his back and forces the knife from his fingers. He throws the knife into a far corner of the room— tauntingly.]

BURKE—Old men is getting childish shouldn't play with knives. [Holding the struggling CHRIS at arm's length—with a sudden rush of anger, drawing back his fist.] I've half a mind to hit you a great clout will put sense in your square head. Kape off me now, I'm warning you! [He gives CHRIS a push with the flat of his hand which sends the old Swede staggering back against the cabin wall, where he remains standing, panting heavily, his eyes fixed on BURKE with hatred, as if he were only collecting his strength to rush at him again.]

BURKE—[Warningly.] Now don't be coming at me again, I'm saying, or I'll flatten you on the floor with a blow, if 'tis Anna's father you are itself! I've no patience left for you. [Then with an amused laugh.] Well, 'tis a bold old man you are just the same, and I'd never think it was in you to come tackling me alone. [A shadow crosses the cabin windows. Both men start. ANNA appears in the doorway.]

ANNA—[With pleased surprise as she sees BURKE.] Hello, Mat. Are you here already? I was down—[She stops, looking from one to the other, sensing immediately that something has happened.] What's up? [Then noticing the overturned chair—in alarm.] How'd that chair get knocked over? [Turning on BURKE reproachfully.] You ain't been fighting with him, Mat—after you promised?

BURKE—[His old self again.] I've not laid a hand on him, Anna. [He goes and picks up the chair, then turning on the still questioning ANNA—with a reassuring smile.] Let you not be worried at all. 'Twas only a bit of an argument we was having to pass the time till you'd come.

ANNA—It must have been some argument when you got to throwing chairs. [She turns on CHRIS.] Why don't you say something? What was it about?

CHRIS—[Relaxing at last—avoiding her eyes—sheepishly.] Ve vas talking about ships and fallars on sea.

ANNA—[With a relieved smile.] Oh—the old stuff, eh?

BURKE—[Suddenly seeming to come to a bold decision—with a defiant grin at CHRIS.] He's not after telling you the whole of it. We was arguing about you mostly.

54

ANNA—[With a frown.] About me?

BURKE—And we'll be finishing it out right here and now in your presence if you're willing. [He sits down at the left of table.]

ANNA—[Uncertainly—looking from him to her father.] Sure. Tell me what it's all about.

CHRIS—[Advancing toward the table—protesting to BURKE.] No! You don't do dat, you! You tal him you don't vant for hear him talk, Anna.

ANNA—But I do. I want this cleared up.

CHRIS—[Miserably afraid now.] Vell, not now, anyvay. You vas going ashore, yes? You ain't got time—

ANNA—[Firmly.] Yes, right here and now. [She turns to BURKE.] You tell me, Mat, since he don't want to.

BURKE—[Draws a deep breath—then plunges in boldly.] The whole of it's in a few words only. So's he'd make no mistake, and him hating the sight of me, I told him in his teeth I loved you. [Passionately.] And that's God truth, Anna, and well you know it!

CHRIS—[Scornfully—forcing a laugh.] Ho-ho! He tal same tang to gel every port he go!

ANNA—[Shrinking from her father with repulsion—resentfully.] Shut up, can't you? [Then to BURKE—feelingly.] I know it's true, Mat. I don't mind what he says.

BURKE—[Humbly grateful.] God bless you!

ANNA—And then what?

BURKE—And then—[Hesitatingly.] And then I said—[He looks at her pleadingly.] I said I was sure—I told him I thought you have a bit of love for me, too. [Passionately.] Say you do, Anna! Let you not destroy me entirely, for the love of God! [He grasps both her hands in his two.]

55

ANNA—[Deeply moved and troubled—forcing a trembling laugh.] So you told him that, Mat? No wonder he was mad. [Forcing out the words.] Well, maybe it's true, Mat. Maybe I do. I been thinking and thinking—I didn't want to, Mat, I'll own up to that—I tried to cut it out—but—[She laughs helplessly.] I guess I can't help it anyhow. So I guess I do, Mat. [Then with a sudden joyous defiance.] Sure I do! What's the use of kidding myself different? Sure I love you, Mat!

CHRIS—[With a cry of pain.] Anna! [He sits crushed.]

BURKE—[With a great depth of sincerity in his humble gratitude.] God be praised!

ANNA—[Assertively.] And I ain't never loved a man in my life before, you can always believe that—no matter what happens.

BURKE—[Goes over to her and puts his arms around her.] Sure I do be believing ivery word you iver said or iver will say. And 'tis you and me will be having a grand, beautiful life together to the end of our days! [He tries to kiss her. At first she turns away her head—then, overcome by a fierce impulse of passionate love, she takes his head in both her hands and holds his face close to hers, staring into his eyes. Then she kisses him full on the lips.]

ANNA—[Pushing him away from her—forcing a broken laugh.] Good-bye. [She walks to the doorway in rear—stands with her back toward them, looking out. Her shoulders quiver once or twice as if she were fighting back her sobs.]

BURKE—[Too in the seventh heaven of bliss to get any correct interpretation of her word—with a laugh.] Good-bye, is it? The divil you say! I'll be coming back at you in a second for more of the same! [To CHRIS, who has quickened to instant attention at his daughter's good-bye, and has looked back at her with a stirring of foolish hope in his eyes.] Now, me old bucko, what'll you be saying? You heard the words from her own lips. Confess I've bate you. Own up like a man when you're bate fair and square. And here's my hand to you—[Holds out his hand.] And let you take it and we'll shake and forget what's over and done, and be friends from this out.

CHRIS—[With implacable hatred.] Ay don't shake hands vith you fallar—not vhile Ay live!

BURKE—[Offended.] The back of my hand to you then, if that suits you better. [Growling.] 'Tis a rotten bad loser you are, divil mend you!

CHRIS—Ay don't lose—[Trying to be scornful and self-convincing.] Anna say she like you little bit but you don't hear her say she marry you, Ay bet. [At the sound of her name ANNA has turned round to them. Her face is composed and calm again, but it is the dead calm of despair.]

BURKE—[Scornfully.] No, and I wasn't hearing her say the sun is shining either.

CHRIS—[Doggedly.] Dat's all right. She don't say it, yust same.

ANNA—[Quietly—coming forward to them.] No, I didn't say it, Mat.

CHRIS—[Eagerly.] Dere! You hear!

BURKE—[Misunderstanding her—with a grin.] You're waiting till you do be asked, you mane? Well, I'm asking you now. And we'll be married this day, with the help of God!

ANNA—[Gently.] You heard what I said, Mat—after I kissed you?

BURKE—[Alarmed by something in her manner.] No—I disremember.

ANNA—I said good-bye. [Her voice trembling.] That kiss was for good-bye, Mat.

BURKE—[Terrified.] What d'you mane?

ANNA—I can't marry you, Mat—and we've said good-bye. That's all.

57

CHRIS—[Unable to hold back his exultation.] Ay know it! Ay know dat vas so!

BURKE—[Jumping to his feet—unable to believe his ears.] Anna! Is it making game of me you'd be? 'Tis a quare time to joke with me, and don't be doing it, for the love of God.

ANNA—[Looking him in the eyes—steadily.] D'you think I'd kid you now? No, I'm not joking, Mat. I mean what I said.

BURKE—Ye don't! Ye can't! 'Tis mad you are. I'm telling you!

ANNA—[Fixedly.] No I'm not.

BURKE—[Desperately.] But what's come over you so sudden? You was saying you loved me—

ANNA—I'll say that as often as you want me to. It's true.

BURKE—[Bewilderedly.] Then why—what, in the divil's name—Oh, God help me, I can't make head or tail to it at all!

ANNA—Because it's the best way out I can figure, Mat. [Her voice catching.] I been thinking it over and thinking it over day and night all week. Don't think it ain't hard on me, too, Mat.

BURKE—For the love of God, tell me then, what is it that's preventing you wedding me when the two of us has love? [Suddenly getting an idea and pointing at CHRIS—exasperatedly.] Is it giving heed to the like of that old fool ye are, and him hating me and filling your ears full of bloody lies against me?

CHRIS—[Getting to his feet—raging triumphantly before ANNA has a chance to get in a word.] Yes, Anna believe me, not you! She know her old fa'der don't lie like you.

ANNA—[Turning on her father angrily.] You sit down, d'you hear? Where do you come in butting in and making things worse? You're like a devil, you are! [Harshly.] Good Lord, and I was beginning to like you, beginning to forget all I've got held up against you!

58

CHRIS—[Crushed—feebly.] You ain't got nutting for hold against me, Anna.

ANNA—Ain't I yust! Well, lemme tell you—[She glances at BURKE and stops abruptly.] Say, Mat, I'm s'prised at you. You didn't think anything he'd said—

BURKE—[Glumly.] Sure, what else would it be?

ANNA—Think I've ever paid any attention to all his crazy bull? Gee, you must take me for a five-year-old kid.

BURKE—[Puzzled and beginning to be irritated at her too.] I don't know how to take you, with your saying this one minute and that the next.

ANNA—Well, he has nothing to do with it.

BURKE—Then what is it has? Tell me, and don't keep me waiting and sweating blood.

ANNA—[Resolutely] I can't tell you—and I won't. I got a good reason—and that's all you need to know. I can't marry you, that's all there is to it. [Distractedly.] So, for Gawd's sake, let's talk of something else.

BURKE—I'll not! [Then fearfully.] Is it married to someone else you are—in the West maybe?

ANNA—[Vehemently.] I should say not.

BURKE—[Regaining his courage.] To the divil with all other reasons then. They don't matter with me at all. [He gets to his feet confidently, assuming a masterful tone.] I'm thinking you're the like of them women can't make up their mind till they're drove to it. Well, then, I'll make up your mind for you bloody quick. [He takes her by the arms, grinning to soften his serious bullying.] We've had enough of talk! Let you be going into your room now and be dressing in your best and we'll be going ashore.

59

CHRIS—[Aroused—angrily.] No, py God, she don't do that! [Takes hold of her arm.]

ANNA—[Who has listened to BURKE in astonishment. She draws away from him, instinctively repelled by his tone, but not exactly sure if he is serious or not—a trace of resentment in her voice.] Say, where do you get that stuff?

BURKE—[Imperiously.] Never mind, now! Let you go get dressed, I'm saying, [Then turning to CHRIS.] We'll be seeing who'll win in the end—me or you.

CHRIS—[To ANNA—also in an authoritative tone.] You stay right here, Anna, you hear! [ANNA stands looking from one to the other of them as if she thought they had both gone crazy. Then the expression of her face freezes into the hardened sneer of her experience.]

BURKE—[Violently.] She'll not! She'll do what I say! You've had your hold on her long enough. It's my turn now.

ANNA—[With a hard laugh.] Your turn? Say, what am I, anyway?

BURKE—'Tis not what you are, 'tis what you're going to be this day—and that's wedded to me before night comes. Hurry up now with your dressing.

CHRIS—[Commandingly.] You don't do one tang he say, Anna! [ANNA laughs mockingly.]

BURKE—She will, so!

CHRIS—Ay tal you she don't! Ay'm her fa'der.

BURKE—She will in spite of you. She's taking my orders from this out, not yours.

ANNA—[Laughing again.] Orders is good!

BURKE—[Turning to her impatiently.] Hurry up now, and shake a

60

leg. We've no time to be wasting. [Irritated as she doesn't move.] Do you hear what I'm telling you?

CHRIS—You stay dere, Anna!

ANNA—[At the end of her patience—blazing out at them passionately.] You can go to hell, both of you! [There is something in her tone that makes them forget their quarrel and turn to her in a stunned amazement. ANNA laughs wildly.] You're just like all the rest of them—you two! Gawd, you'd think I was a piece of furniture! I'll show you! Sit down now! [As they hesitate—furiously.] Sit down and let me talk for a minute. You're all wrong, see? Listen to me! I'm going to tell you something—and then I'm going to beat it. [To BURKE—with a harsh laugh.] I'm going to tell you a funny story, so pay attention. [Pointing to CHRIS.] I've been meaning to turn it loose on him every time he'd get my goat with his bull about keeping me safe inland. I wasn't going to tell you, but you've forced me into it. What's the dif? It's all wrong anyway, and you might as well get cured that way as any other. [With hard mocking.] Only don't forget what you said a minute ago about it not mattering to you what other reason I got so long as I wasn't married to no one else.

BURKE—[Manfully.] That's my word, and I'll stick to it!

ANNA—[Laughing bitterly.] What a chance! You make me laugh, honest! Want to bet you will? Wait 'n see! [She stands at the table rear, looking from one to the other of the two men with her hard, mocking smile. Then she begins, fighting to control her emotion and speak calmly.] First thing is, I want to tell you two guys something. You was going on's if one of you had got to own me. But nobody owns me, see?—'cepting myself. I'll do what I please and no man, I don't give a hoot who he is, can tell me what to do! I ain't asking either of you for a living. I can make it myself—one way or other. I'm my own boss. So put that in your pipe and smoke it! You and your orders!

BURKE—[Protestingly.] I wasn't meaning it that way at all and well

61

you know it. You've no call to be raising this rumpus with me. [Pointing to CHRIS.] 'Tis him you've a right—

ANNA—I'm coming to him. But you—you did mean it that way, too. You sounded—yust like all the rest. [Hysterically.] But, damn it, shut up! Let me talk for a change!

BURKE—'Tis quare, rough talk, that—for a dacent girl the like of you!

ANNA—[With a hard laugh.] Decent? Who told you I was? [CHRIS is sitting with bowed shoulders, his head in his hands. She leans over in exasperation and shakes him violently by the shoulder.] Don't go to sleep, Old Man! Listen here, I'm talking to you now!

CHRIS—[Straightening up and looking about as if he were seeking a way to escape—with frightened foreboding in his voice.] Ay don't vant for hear it. You vas going out of head, Ay tank, Anna.

ANNA—[Violently.] Well, living with you is enough to drive anyone off their nut. Your bunk about the farm being so fine! Didn't I write you year after year how rotten it was and what a dirty slave them cousins made of me? What'd you care? Nothing! Not even enough to come out and see me! That crazy bull about wanting to keep me away from the sea don't go down with me! You yust didn't want to be bothered with me! You're like all the rest of 'em!

CHRIS—[Feebly.] Anna! It ain't so—

ANNA—[Not heeding his interruption—revengefully.] But one thing I never wrote you. It was one of them cousins that you think is such nice people—the youngest son—Paul—that started me wrong. [Loudly.] It wasn't none of my fault. I hated him worse 'n hell and he knew it. But he was big and strong—[Pointing to Burke]—like you!

BURKE—[Half springing to his feet—his fists clenched,] God blarst it! [He sinks slowly back in his chair again, the knuckles showing white on his clenched hands, his face tense with the effort to suppress his grief and rage.]

CHRIS—[In a cry of horrified pain.] Anna!

ANNA—[To him—seeming not to have heard their interruptions.] That was why I run away from the farm. That was what made me get a yob as nurse girl in St. Paul. [With a hard, mocking laugh.] And you think that was a nice yob for a girl, too, don't you? [Sarcastically.] With all them nice inland fellers yust looking for a chance to marry me, I s'pose. Marry me? What a chance! They wasn't looking for marrying. [As BURKE lets a groan of fury escape him—desperately.] I'm owning up to everything fair and square. I was caged in, I tell you—yust like in yail—taking care of other people's kids—listening to 'em bawling and crying day and night—when I wanted to be out—and I was lonesome—lonesome as hell! [With a sudden weariness in her voice.] So I give up finally. What was the use? [She stops and looks at the two men. Both are motionless and silent. CHRIS seems in a stupor of despair, his house of cards fallen about him. BURKE's face is livid with the rage that is eating him up, but he is too stunned and bewildered yet to find a vent for it. The condemnation she feels in their silence goads ANNA into a harsh, strident defiance.] You don't say nothing—either of you—but I know what you're thinking. You're like all the rest! [To CHRIS—furiously.] And who's to blame for it, me or you? If you'd even acted like a man—if you'd even been a regular father and had me with you—maybe things would be different!

CHRIS—[In agony.] Don't talk dat vay, Anna! Ay go crazy! Ay von't listen! [Puts his hands over his ears.]

ANNA—[Infuriated by his action—stridently.] You will too listen! [She leans over and pulls his hands from his ears—with hysterical rage.] You—keeping me safe inland—I wasn't no nurse girl the last two years—I lied when I wrote you—I was in a house, that's what!—yes, that kind of a house—the kind sailors like you and Mat goes to in port—and your nice inland men, too—and all men, God damn 'em! I hate 'em! Hate 'em! [She breaks into hysterical sobbing, throwing herself into the chair and hiding her face in her hands on the table. The two men have sprung to their feet.]

63

CHRIS—[Whimpering like a child.] Anna! Anna! It's lie! It's lie! [He stands wringing his hands together and begins to weep.]

BURKE—[His whole great body tense like a spring—dully and gropingly.] So that's what's in it!

ANNA—[Raising her head at the sound of his voice—with extreme mocking bitterness.] I s'pose you remember your promise, Mat? No other reason was to count with you so long as I wasn't married already. So I s'pose you want me to get dressed and go ashore, don't you? [She laughs.] Yes, you do!

BURKE—[On the verge of his outbreak—stammeringly.] God stiffen you!

ANNA—[Trying to keep up her hard, bitter tone, but gradually letting a note of pitiful pleading creep in.] I s'pose if I tried to tell you I wasn't—that—no more you'd believe me, wouldn't you? Yes, you would! And if I told you that yust getting out in this barge, and being on the sea had changed me and made me feel different about things,'s if all I'd been through wasn't me and didn't count and was yust like it never happened—you'd laugh, wouldn't you? And you'd die laughing sure if I said that meeting you that funny way that night in the fog, and afterwards seeing that you was straight goods stuck on me, had got me to thinking for the first time, and I sized you up as a different kind of man—a sea man as different from the ones on land as water is from mud—and that was why I got stuck on you, too. I wanted to marry you and fool you, but I couldn't. Don't you see how I'd changed? I couldn't marry you with you believing a lie—and I was shamed to tell you the truth—till the both of you forced my hand, and I seen you was the same as all the rest. And now, give me a bawling out and beat it, like I can tell you're going to. [She stops, looking at BURKE. He is silent, his face averted, his features beginning to work with fury. She pleads passionately.] Will you believe it if I tell you that loving you has made me—clean? It's the straight goods, honest! [Then as he doesn't reply—bitterly.] Like hell you will! You're like all the rest!

64

BURKE—[Blazing out—turning on her in a perfect frenzy of rage—his voice trembling with passion.] The rest, is it? God's curse on you! Clane, is it? You slut, you, I'll be killing you now! [He picks up the chair on which he has been sitting and, swinging it high over his shoulder, springs toward her. CHRIS rushes forward with a cry of alarm, trying to ward off the blow from his daughter. ANNA looks up into BURKE'S eyes with the fearlessness of despair. BURKE checks himself, the chair held in the air.]

CHRIS—[Wildly.] Stop, you crazy fool! You vant for murder her!

ANNA—[Pushing her father away brusquely, her eyes still holding BURKE'S.] Keep out of this, you! [To BURKE—dully.] Well, ain't you got the nerve to do it? Go ahead! I'll be thankful to you, honest. I'm sick of the whole game.

BURKE—[Throwing the chair away into a corner of the room—helplessly.] I can't do it, God help me, and your two eyes looking at me. [Furiously.] Though I do be thinking I'd have a good right to smash your skull like a rotten egg. Was there iver a woman in the world had the rottenness in her that you have, and was there iver a man the like of me was made the fool of the world, and me thinking thoughts about you, and having great love for you, and dreaming dreams of the fine life we'd have when we'd be wedded! [His voice high pitched in a lamentation that is like a keen]. Yerra, God help me! I'm destroyed entirely and my heart is broken in bits! I'm asking God Himself, was it for this He'd have me roaming the earth since I was a lad only, to come to black shame in the end, where I'd be giving a power of love to a woman is the same as others you'd meet in any hooker-shanty in port, with red gowns on them and paint on their grinning mugs, would be sleeping with any man for a dollar or two!

ANNA—[In a scream.] Don't, Mat! For Gawd's sake! [Then raging and pounding on the table with her hands.] Get out of here! Leave me alone! Get out of here!

BURKE—[His anger rushing back on him.] I'll be going, surely!

And I'll be drinking sloos of whiskey will wash that black kiss of yours off my lips; and I'll be getting dead rotten drunk so I'll not remember if 'twas iver born you was at all; and I'll be shipping away on some boat will take me to the other end of the world where I'll never see your face again! [He turns toward the door]

CHRIS—[Who has been standing in a stupor—suddenly grasping BURKE by the arm—stupidly] No, you don't go. Ay tank maybe it's better Anna marry you now.

BURKE—[Shaking CHRIS off—furiously] Lave go of me, ye old ape! Marry her, is it? I'd see her roasting in hell first! I'm shipping away out of this, I'm telling you! [Pointing to Anna—passionately] And my curse on you and the curse of Almighty God and all the Saints! You've destroyed me this day and may you lie awake in the long nights, tormented with thoughts of Mat Burke and the great wrong you've done him!

ANNA—[In anguish] Mat! [But he turns without another word and strides out of the doorway. ANNA looks after him wildly, starts to run after him, then hides her face in her outstretched arms, sobbing. CHRIS stands in a stupor, staring at the floor.]

CHRIS—[After a pause, dully.] Ay tank Ay go ashore, too.

ANNA—[Looking up, wildly.] Not after him! Let him go! Don't you dare—

CHRIS—[Somberly.] Ay go for gat drink.

ANNA—[With a harsh laugh.] So I'm driving you to drink, too, eh? I s'pose you want to get drunk so's you can forget—like him?

CHRIS—[Bursting out angrily.] Yes, Ay vant! You tank Ay like hear dem tangs. [Breaking down—weeping.] Ay tank you vasn't dat kind of gel, Anna.

ANNA—[Mockingly.] And I s'pose you want me to beat it, don't you? You don't want me here disgracing you, I s'pose?

66

CHRIS—No, you stay here! [Goes over and pats her on the shoulder, the tears running down his face.] Ain't your fault, Anna, Ay know dat. [She looks up at him, softened. He bursts into rage.] It's dat ole davil, sea, do this to me! [He shakes his fist at the door.] It's her dirty tricks! It vas all right on barge with yust you and me. Den she bring dat Irish fallar in fog, she make you like him, she make you fight with me all time! If dat Irish fallar don't never come, you don't never tal me dem tangs, Ay don't never know, and every tang's all right. [He shakes his fist again,] Dirty ole davil!

ANNA—[With spent weariness.] Oh, what's the use? Go on ashore and get drunk.

CHRIS—[Goes into room on left and gets his cap. He goes to the door, silent and stupid—then turns.] You vait here, Anna?

ANNA—[Dully] Maybe—and maybe not. Maybe I'll get drunk, too. Maybe I'll—But what the hell do you care what I do? Go on and beat it. [CHRIS turns stupidly and goes out. ANNA sits at the table, staring straight in front of her.]

[The Curtain Falls]

ACT IV

SCENE—Same as Act Three, about nine o'clock of a foggy night two days later. The whistles of steamers in the harbor can be heard. The cabin is lighted by a small lamp on the table. A suitcase stands in the middle of the floor. ANNA is sitting in the rocking-chair. She wears a hat, is all dressed up as in Act One. Her face is pale, looks terribly tired and worn, as if the two days just past had been ones of suffering and sleepless nights. She stares before her despondently, her chin in her hands. There is a timid knock on the door in rear. ANNA jumps to her feet with a startled exclamation and looks toward the door with an expression of mingled hope and fear.

ANNA—[Faintly.] Come in. [Then summoning her courage—more resolutely.] Come in. [The door is opened and CHRIS appears in the doorway. He is in a very bleary, bedraggled condition, suffering from the after effects of his drunk. A tin pail full of foaming beer is in his hand. He comes forward, his eyes avoiding ANNA'S. He mutters stupidly.] It's foggy.

ANNA—[Looking him over with contempt.] So you come back at last, did you? You're a fine looking sight! [Then jeeringly.] I thought you'd beaten it for good on account of the disgrace I'd brought on you.

CHRIS—[Wincing-faintly.] Don't say dat, Anna, please! [He sits in a chair by the table, setting down the can of beer, holding his head in his hands]

ANNA—[Looks at him with a certain sympathy.] What's the trouble? Feeling sick?

CHRIS—[Dully.] Inside my head feel sick.

68

ANNA—Well, what d'you expect after being soused for two days? [Resentfully.] It serves you right. A fine thing—you leaving me alone on this barge all that time!

CHRIS—[Humbly.] Ay'm sorry, Anna.

ANNA—[Scornfully.] Sorry!

CHRIS—But Ay'm not sick inside head vay you mean. Ay'm sick from tank too much about you, about me.

ANNA—And how about me? D'you suppose I ain't been thinking, too?

CHRIS—Ay'm sorry, Anna. [He sees her bag and gives a start] You pack your bag, Anna? You vas going—?

ANNA—[Forcibly.] Yes, I was going right back to what you think.

CHRIS—Anna!

ANNA—I went ashore to get a train for New York. I'd been waiting and waiting 'till I was sick of it. Then I changed my mind and decided not to go to-day. But I'm going first thing to-morrow, so it'll all be the same in the end.

CHRIS—[Raising his head—pleadingly] No, you never do dat, Anna!

ANNA—[With a sneer.] Why not, I'd like to know?

CHRIS—You don't never gat to do—dat vay—no more, Ay tal you. Ay fix dat up all right.

ANNA—[Suspiciously.] Fix what up?

CHRIS—[Not seeming to have heard her question—sadly.] You vas vaiting, you say? You vasn't vaiting for me, Ay bet.

ANNA—[Callously.] You'd win.

69

CHRIS—For dat Irish fallar?

ANNA—[Defiantly.] Yes—if you want to know! [Then with a forlorn laugh.] If he did come back it'd only because he wanted to beat me up or kill me, I suppose. But even if he did, I'd rather have him come than not show up at all. I wouldn't care what he did.

CHRIS—Ay guess it's true you vas in love with him all right.

ANNA—You guess!

CHRIS—[Turning to her earnestly.] And Ay'm sorry for you like hell he don't come, Anna!

ANNA—[Softened.] Seems to me you've changed your tune a lot.

CHRIS—Ay've been tanking, and Ay guess it vas all my fault—all bad tangs dat happen to you. [Pleadingly.] You try for not hate me, Anna. Ay'm crazy ole fool, dat's all.

ANNA—Who said I hated you?

CHRIS—Ay'm sorry for everytang Ay do wrong for you, Anna. Ay vant for you be happy all rest of your life for make up! It make you happy marry dat Irish fallar, Ay vant it, too.

ANNA—[Dully.]—Well, there ain't no chance. But I'm glad you think different about it, anyway.

CHRIS—[Supplicatingly.] And you tank—maybe—you forgive me sometime?

ANNA—[With a wan smile.] I'll forgive you right now.

CHRIS—[Seizing her hand and kissing it—brokenly.] Anna lilla! Anna lilla!

ANNA—[Touched but a bit embarrassed.] Don't bawl about it. There ain't nothing to forgive, anyway. It ain't your fault, and it ain't mine, and it ain't his neither. We're all poor nuts, and things happen, and we yust get mixed in wrong, that's all.

70

CHRIS—[Eagerly.] You say right tang, Anna, py golly! It ain't nobody's fault! [Shaking his fist.] It's dat ole davil, sea!

ANNA—[With an exasperated laugh.] Gee, won't you ever can that stuff? [CHRIS relapses into injured silence. After a pause ANNA continues curiously.] You said a minute ago you'd fixed something up—about me. What was it?

CHRIS—[After a hesitating pause.] Ay'm shipping avay on sea again, Anna.

ANNA—[Astounded.] You're—what?

CHRIS—Ay sign on steamer sail to-morrow. Ay gat my ole yob—bo'sun. [ANNA stares at him. As he goes on, a bitter smile comes over her face.] Ay tank dat's best tang for you. Ay only bring you bad luck, Ay tank. Ay make your mo'der's life sorry. Ay don't vant make yours dat way, but Ay do yust same. Dat ole davil, sea, she make me Yonah man ain't no good for nobody. And Ay tank now it ain't no use fight with sea. No man dat live going to beat her, py yingo!

ANNA—[With a laugh of helpless bitterness.] So that's how you've fixed me, is it?

CHRIS—Yes, Ay tank if dat ole davil gat me back she leave you alone den.

ANNA—[Bitterly.] But, for Gawd's sake, don't you see, you're doing the same thing you've always done? Don't you see—? [But she sees the look of obsessed stubbornness on her father's face and gives it up helplessly.] But what's the use of talking. You ain't right, that's what. I'll never blame you for nothing no more. But how you could figure out that was fixing me—!

CHRIS—Dat ain't all. Ay gat dem fallars in steam-ship office to pay you all money coming to me every month vhile Ay'm avay.

ANNA—[With a hard laugh.] Thanks. But I guess I won't be hard up for no small change.

CHRIS—[Hurt—humbly.] It ain't much, Ay know, but it's plenty for keep you so you never gat go.

ANNA—[Shortly.] Shut up, will you? We'll talk about it later, see?

CHRIS—[After a pause—ingratiatingly.] You like Ay go ashore look for dat Irish fallar, Anna?

ANNA—[Angrily.] Not much! Think I want to drag him back?

CHRIS—[After a pause—uncomfortably.] Py golly, dat booze don't go veil. Give me fever, Ay tank, Ay feel hot like hell. [He takes off his coat and lets it drop on the floor. There is a loud thud.]

ANNA—[With a start.] What you got in your pocket, for Pete's sake—a ton of lead? [She reaches down, takes the coat and pulls out a revolver—looks from it to him in amazement.] A gun? What were you doing with this?

CHRIS—[Sheepishly.] Ay forgat. Ain't nutting. Ain't loaded, anyvay.

ANNA—[Breaking it open to make sure—then closing it again—looking at him suspiciously.] That ain't telling me why you got it?

CHRIS—[Sheepishly.] Ay'm ole fool. Ay gat it vhen Ay go ashore first. Ay tank den it's all fault of dat Irish fallar.

ANNA—[With a shudder.] Say, you're crazier than I thought. I never dreamt you'd go that far.

CHRIS—[Quickly.] Ay don't. Ay gat better sense right avay. Ay don't never buy bullets even. It ain't his fault, Ay know.

ANNA—[Still suspicious of him.] Well, I'll take care of this for a while, loaded or not. [She puts it in the drawer of table and closes the drawer.]

CHRIS—[Placatingly.] Throw it overboard if you vant. Ay don't care, [Then after a pause.] Py golly, Ay tank Ay go lie down. Ay feel sick. [ANNA takes a magazine from the table. CHRIS hesitates by her chair.] Ve talk again before Ay go, yes?

ANNA—[Dully.] Where's this ship going to?

CHRIS—Cape Town. Dat's in South Africa. She's British steamer called Londonderry. [He stands hesitatingly—finally blurts out.] Anna—you forgive me sure?

ANNA—[Wearily.] Sure I do. You ain't to blame. You're yust— what you are—like me.

CHRIS—[Pleadingly.] Den—you lat me kiss you again once?

ANNA—[Raising her face—forcing a wan smile.] Sure. No hard feelings.

CHRIS—[Kisses her—brokenly.] Anna lilla! Ay—[He fights for words to express himself, but finds none—miserably—with a sob.] Ay can't say it. Good-night, Anna.

ANNA—Good-night. [He picks up the can of beer and goes slowly into the room on left, his shoulders bowed, his head sunk forward dejectedly. He closes the door after him. ANNA turns over the pages of the magazine, trying desperately to banish her thoughts by looking at the pictures. This fails to distract her, and flinging the magazine back on the table, she springs to her feet and walks about the cabin distractedly, clenching and unclenching her hands. She speaks aloud to herself in a tense, trembling voice.] Gawd, I can't stand this much longer! What am I waiting for anyway?—like a damn fool! [She laughs helplessly, then checks herself abruptly, as she hears the sound of heavy footsteps on the deck outside. She appears to recognize these and her face lights up with joy. She gasps:] Mat! [A strange terror seems suddenly to seize her. She rushes to the table, takes the revolver out of drawer and crouches down in the corner, left, behind the cupboard. A moment later the door is flung open and MAT BURKE appears in the doorway. He is in bad shape—his clothes torn and dirty, covered with sawdust as if he had been grovelling or sleeping on barroom floors. There is a red bruise on his forehead over one of his eyes, another over one cheekbone, his knuckles are skinned and raw—plain evidence of the fighting he has been through on his "bat." His eyes are bloodshot and heavy-lidded, his face has a bloated look. But beyond these appearances—the results of heavy drinking—there is an expression in his eyes of wild mental turmoil, of impotent animal rage baffled by its own abject misery.]

BURKE—[Peers blinkingly about the cabin—hoarsely.] Let you not be hiding from me, whoever's here—though 'tis well you know I'd have a right to come back and murder you. [He stops to listen. Hearing no sound, he closes the door behind him and comes forward to the table. He throws himself into the rocking-chair—despondently.] There's no one here, I'm thinking, and 'tis a great fool I am to be coming. [With a sort of dumb, uncomprehending anguish.] Yerra, Mat Burke, 'tis a great jackass you've become and what's got into you at all, at all? She's gone out of this long ago, I'm telling you, and you'll never see her face again. [ANNA stands up, hesitating, struggling between joy and fear. BURKE'S eyes fall on ANNA'S bag. He leans over to examine it.] What's this? [Joyfully.] It's hers. She's not gone! But where is she? Ashore? [Darkly.] What would she be doing ashore on this rotten night? [His face suddenly convulsed with grief and rage.] 'Tis that, is it? Oh, God's curse on her! [Raging.] I'll wait 'till she comes and choke her dirty life out. [ANNA starts, her face grows hard. She steps into the room, the revolver in her right hand by her side.]

ANNA—[In a cold, hard tone.] What are you doing here?

BURKE—[Wheeling about with a terrified gasp] Glory be to God! [They remain motionless and silent for a moment, holding each other's eyes.]

ANNA—[In the same hard voice] Well, can't you talk?

BURKE—[Trying to fall into an easy, careless tone] You've a year's growth scared out of me, coming at me so sudden and me thinking I was alone.

ANNA—You've got your nerve butting in here without knocking or nothing. What d'you want?

BURKE—[Airily] Oh, nothing much. I was wanting to have a last word with you, that's all. [He moves a step toward her.]

ANNA—[Sharply—raising the revolver in her hand.] Careful now! Don't try getting too close. I heard what you said you'd do to me.

BURKE—[Noticing the revolver for the first time.] Is it murdering me you'd be now, God forgive you? [Then with a contemptuous laugh.] Or is it thinking I'd be frightened by that old tin whistle? [He walks straight for her.]

ANNA—[Wildly.] Look out, I tell you!

BURKE—[Who has come so close that the revolver is almost touching his chest.] Let you shoot, then! [Then with sudden wild grief.] Let you shoot, I'm saying, and be done with it! Let you end me with a shot and I'll be thanking you, for it's a rotten dog's life I've lived the past two days since I've known what you are, 'til I'm after wishing I was never born at all!

ANNA—[Overcome—letting the revolver drop to the floor, as if her fingers had no strength to hold it—hysterically.] What d'you want coming here? Why don't you beat it? Go on! [She passes him and sinks down in the rocking-chair.]

BURKE—[Following her—mournfully.] 'Tis right you'd be asking why did I come. [Then angrily.] 'Tis because 'tis a great weak fool of the world I am, and me tormented with the wickedness you'd told of yourself, and drinking oceans of booze that'd make me forget. Forget? Divil a word I'd forget, and your face grinning always in front of my eyes, awake or asleep, 'til I do be thinking a madhouse is the proper place for me.

ANNA—[Glancing at his hands and—face—scornfully] You look like you ought to be put away some place. Wonder you wasn't pulled in. You been scrapping, too, ain't you?

75

BURKE—I have—with every scut would take off his coat to me! [Fiercely.] And each time I'd be hitting one a clout in the mug, it wasn't his face I'd be seeing at all, but yours, and me wanting to drive you a blow would knock you out of this world where I wouldn't be seeing or thinking more of you.

ANNA—[Her lips trembling pitifully] Thanks!

BURKE—[Walking up and down—distractedly.] That's right, make game of me! Oh, I'm a great coward surely, to be coming back to speak with you at all. You've a right to laugh at me.

ANNA—I ain't laughing at you, Mat.

BURKE—[Unheeding.] You to be what you are, and me to be Mat Burke, and me to be drove back to look at you again! 'Tis black shame is on me!

ANNA—[Resentfully.] Then get out. No one's holding you!

BURKE—[Bewilderedly] And me to listen to that talk from a woman like you and be frightened to close her mouth with a slap! Oh, God help me, I'm a yellow coward for all men to spit at! [Then furiously] But I'll not be getting out of this 'till I've had me word. [Raising his fist threateningly] And let you look out how you'd drive me! [Letting his fist fall helplessly] Don't be angry now! I'm raving like a real lunatic, I'm thinking, and the sorrow you put on me has my brains drownded in grief. [Suddenly bending down to her and grasping her arm intensely] Tell me it's a lie, I'm saying! That's what I'm after coming to hear you say.

ANNA—[Dully] A lie? What?

BURKE—[With passionate entreaty] All the badness you told me two days back. Sure it must be a lie! You was only making game of me, wasn't you? Tell me 'twas a lie, Anna, and I'll be saying prayers of thanks on my two knees to the Almighty God!

ANNA—[Terribly shaken—faintly.] I can't. Mat. [As he turns away—imploringly.] Oh, Mat, won't you see that no matter what I

76

was I ain't that any more? Why, listen! I packed up my bag this afternoon and went ashore. I'd been waiting here all alone for two days, thinking maybe you'd come back—thinking maybe you'd think over all I'd said—and maybe—oh, I don't know what I was hoping! But I was afraid to even go out of the cabin for a second, honest—afraid you might come and not find me here. Then I gave up hope when you didn't show up and I went to the railroad station. I was going to New York. I was going back—

BURKE—[Hoarsely.] God's curse on you!

ANNA—Listen, Mat! You hadn't come, and I'd gave up hope. But—in the station—I couldn't go. I'd bought my ticket and everything. [She takes the ticket from her dress and tries to hold it before his eyes.] But I got to thinking about you—and I couldn't take the train—I couldn't! So I come back here—to wait some more. Oh, Mat, don't you see I've changed? Can't you forgive what's dead and gone—and forget it?

BURKE—[Turning on her—overcome by rage again.] Forget, is it? I'll not forget 'til my dying day, I'm telling you, and me tormented with thoughts. [In a frenzy.] Oh, I'm wishing I had wan of them fornenst me this minute and I'd beat him with my fists 'till he'd be a bloody corpse! I'm wishing the whole lot of them will roast in hell 'til the Judgment Day—and yourself along with them, for you're as bad as they are.

ANNA—[Shuddering.] Mat! [Then after a pause—in a voice of dead, stony calm.] Well, you've had your say. Now you better beat it.

BURKE—[Starts slowly for the door—hesitates—then after a pause.] And what'll you be doing?

ANNA—What difference does it make to you?

BURKE—I'm asking you!

ANNA—[In the same tone.] My bag's packed and I got my ticket. I'll go to New York to-morrow.

77

BURKE—[Helplessly.] You mean—you'll be doing the same again?

ANNA—[Stonily.] Yes.

BURKE—[In anguish.] You'll not! Don't torment me with that talk! 'Tis a she-divil you are sent to drive me mad entirely!

ANNA—[Her voice breaking.] Oh, for Gawd's sake, Mat, leave me alone! Go away! Don't you see I'm licked? Why d'you want to keep on kicking me?

BURKE—[Indignantly.] And don't you deserve the worst I'd say, God forgive you?

ANNA—All right. Maybe I do. But don't rub it in. Why ain't you done what you said you was going to? Why ain't you got that ship was going to take you to the other side of the earth where you'd never see me again?

BURKE—I have.

ANNA—[Startled.] What—then you're going—honest?

BURKE—I signed on to-day at noon, drunk as I was—and she's sailing to-morrow.

ANNA—And where's she going to?

BURKE—Cape Town.

ANNA—[The memory of having heard that name a little while before coming to her—with a start, confusedly.] Cape Town? Where's that. Far away?

BURKE—'Tis at the end of Africa. That's far for you.

ANNA—[Forcing a laugh.] You're keeping your word all right, ain't you? [After a slight pause—curiously.] What's the boat's name?

BURKE—The Londonderry.

78

ANNA—[It suddenly comes to her that this is the same ship her father is sailing on.] The Londonderry! It's the same—Oh, this is too much! [With wild, ironical laughter.] Ha-ha-ha!

BURKE—What's up with you now?

ANNA—Ha-ha-ha! It's funny, funny! I'll die laughing!

BURKE—[Irritated.] Laughing at what?

ANNA—It's a secret. You'll know soon enough. It's funny. [Controlling herself—after a pause—cynically.] What kind of a place is this Cape Town? Plenty of dames there, I suppose?

BURKE—To hell with them! That I may never see another woman to my dying hour!

ANNA—That's what you say now, but I'll bet by the time you get there you'll have forgot all about me and start in talking the same old bull you talked to me to the first one you meet.

BURKE—[Offended.] I'll not, then! God mend you, is it making me out to be the like of yourself you are, and you taking up with this one and that all the years of your life?

ANNA—[Angrily assertive.] Yes, that's yust what I do mean! You been doing the same thing all your life, picking up a new girl in every port. How're you any better than I was?

BURKE—[Thoroughly exasperated.] Is it no shame you have at all? I'm a fool to be wasting talk on you and you hardened in badness. I'll go out of this and lave you alone forever. [He starts for the door—then stops to turn on her furiously] And I suppose 'tis the same lies you told them all before that you told to me?

ANNA—[Indignantly.] That's a lie! I never did!

BURKE—[Miserably.] You'd be saying that, anyway.

ANNA—[Forcibly, with growing intensity.] Are you trying to accuse me—of being in love—really in love—with them?
79

BURKE—I'm thinking you were, surely.

ANNA—[Furiously, as if this were the last insult—advancing on him threateningly] You mutt, you! I've stood enough from you. Don't you dare. [With scornful bitterness.] Love 'em! Oh, my Gawd! You damn thick-head! Love 'em? [Savagely.] I hated 'em, I tell you! Hated 'em, hated 'em, hated 'em! And may Gawd strike me dead this minute and my mother, too, if she was alive, if I ain't telling you the honest truth!

BURKE—[Immensely pleased by her vehemence—a light beginning to break over his face—but still uncertain, torn between doubt and the desire to believe—helplessly.] If I could only be believing you now!

ANNA—[Distractedly.] Oh, what's the use? What's the use of me talking? What's the use of anything? [Pleadingly.] Oh, Mat, you mustn't think that for a second! You mustn't! Think all the other bad about me you want to, and I won't kick, 'cause you've a right to. But don't think that! [On the point of tears.] I couldn't bear it! It'd be yust too much to know you was going away where I'd never see you again—thinking that about me!

BURKE—[After an inward struggle—tensely—forcing out the words with difficulty.] If I was believing—that you'd never had love for any other man in the world but me—I could be forgetting the rest, maybe.

ANNA—[With a cry of joy.] Mat!

BURKE—[Slowly.] If 'tis truth you're after telling, I'd have a right, maybe, to believe you'd changed—and that I'd changed you myself 'til the thing you'd been all your life wouldn't be you any more at all.

ANNA—[Hanging on his words—breathlessly.] Oh, Mat! That's what I been trying to tell you all along!

BURKE—[Simply.] For I've a power of strength in me to lead men

80

the way I want, and women, too, maybe, and I'm thinking I'd change you to a new woman entirely, so I'd never know, or you either, what kind of woman you'd been in the past at all.

ANNA—Yes, you could, Mat! I know you could!

BURKE—And I'm thinking 'twasn't your fault, maybe, but having that old ape for a father that left you to grow up alone, made you what you was. And if I could be believing 'tis only me you—

ANNA—[Distractedly.] You got to believe it. Mat! What can I do? I'll do anything, anything you want to prove I'm not lying!

BURKE—[Suddenly seems to have a solution. He feels in the pocket of his coat and grasps something—solemnly.] Would you be willing to swear an oath, now—a terrible, fearful oath would send your soul to the divils in hell if you was lying?

ANNA—[Eagerly.] Sure, I'll swear, Mat—on anything!

BURKE—[Takes a small, cheap old crucifix from his pocket and holds it up for her to see.] Will you swear on this?

ANNA—[Reaching out for it.] Yes. Sure I will. Give it to me.

BURKE—[Holding it away.] 'Tis a cross was given me by my mother, God rest her soul. [He makes the sign of the cross mechanically.] I was a lad only, and she told me to keep it by me if I'd be waking or sleeping and never lose it, and it'd bring me luck. She died soon after. But I'm after keeping it with me from that day to this, and I'm telling you there's great power in it, and 'tis great bad luck it's saved me from and me roaming the seas, and I having it tied round my neck when my last ship sunk, and it bringing me safe to land when the others went to their death. [Very earnestly.] And I'm warning you now, if you'd swear an oath on this, 'tis my old woman herself will be looking down from Hivin above, and praying Almighty God and the Saints to put a great curse on you if she'd hear you swearing a lie!

ANNA—[Awed by his manner—superstitiously] I wouldn't have

81

the nerve—honest—if it was a lie. But it's the truth and I ain't scared to swear. Give it to me.

BURKE—[Handing it to her—almost frightenedly, as if he feared for her safety.] Be careful what you'd swear, I'm saying.

ANNA—[Holding the cross gingerly.] Well—what do you want me to swear? You say it.

BURKE—Swear I'm the only man in the world ivir you felt love for.

ANNA—[Looking into his eyes steadily] I swear it.

BURKE—And that you'll be forgetting from this day all the badness you've done and never do the like of it again.

ANNA—[Forcibly.] I swear it! I swear it by God!

BURKE—And may the blackest curse of God strike you if you're lying. Say it now!

ANNA—And may the blackest curse of God strike me if I'm lying!

BURKE—[With a stupendous sigh.] Oh, glory be to God, I'm after believing you now! [He takes the cross from her hand, his face beaming with joy, and puts it back in his pocket. He puts his arm about her waist and is about to kiss her when he stops, appalled by some terrible doubt.]

ANNA—[Alarmed.] What's the matter with you?

BURKE—[With sudden fierce questioning.] Is it Catholic ye are?

ANNA—[Confused.] No. Why?

BURKE—[Filled with a sort of bewildered foreboding.] Oh, God, help me! [With a dark glance of suspicion at her.] There's some divil's trickery in it, to be swearing an oath on a Catholic cross and you wan of the others.

ANNA—[Distractedly.] Oh, Mat, don't you believe me?

82

BURKE—[Miserably.] If it isn't a Catholic you are—

ANNA—I ain't nothing. What's the difference? Didn't you hear me swear?

BURKE—[Passionately.] Oh, I'd a right to stay away from you—but I couldn't! I was loving you in spite of it all and wanting to be with you, God forgive me, no matter what you are. I'd go mad if I'd not have you! I'd be killing the world—[He seizes her in his arms and kisses her fiercely.]

ANNA—[With a gasp of joy.] Mat!

BURKE—[Suddenly holding her away from him and staring into her eyes as if to probe into her soul—slowly.] If your oath is no proper oath at all, I'll have to be taking your naked word for it and have you anyway, I'm thinking—I'm needing you that bad!

ANNA—[Hurt—reproachfully.] Mat! I swore, didn't I?

BURKE—[Defiantly, as if challenging fate.] Oath or no oath, 'tis no matter. We'll be wedded in the morning, with the help of God. [Still more defiantly.] We'll be happy now, the two of us, in spite of the divil! [He crushes her to him and kisses her again. The door on the left is pushed open and CHRIS appears in the doorway. He stands blinking at them. At first the old expression of hatred of BURKE comes into his eyes instinctively. Then a look of resignation and relief takes its place. His face lights up with a sudden happy thought. He turns back into the bedroom—reappears immediately with the tin can of beer in his hand grinning.]

CHRIS—Me have drink on this, py golly! [They break away from each other with startled exclamations.]

BURKE—[Explosively.] God stiffen it! [He takes a step toward CHRIS threateningly.]

ANNA—[Happily—to her father.] That's the way to talk! [With a laugh.] And say, it's about time for you and Mat to kiss and make up. You're going to be shipmates on the Londonderry, did you know it?

BURKE—[Astounded.] Shipmates—Has himself—

CHRIS—[Equally astounded.] Ay vas bo'sun on her.

BURKE—The divil! [Then angrily.] You'd be going back to sea and leaving her alone, would you?

ANNA—[Quickly.] It's all right, Mat. That's where he belongs, and I want him to go. You got to go, too; we'll need the money. [With a laugh, as she gets the glasses.] And as for me being alone, that runs in the family, and I'll get used to it. [Pouring out their glasses.] I'll get a little house somewhere and I'll make a regular place for you two to come back to,—wait and see. And now you drink up and be friends.

BURKE—[Happily—but still a bit resentful against the old man.] Sure! [Clinking his glass against CHRIS'.] Here's luck to you! [He drinks.]

CHRIS—[Subdued—his face melancholy.] Skoal. [He drinks.]

BURKE—[To Anna, with a wink.] You'll not be lonesome long. I'll see to that, with the help of God. 'Tis himself here will be having a grandchild to ride on his foot, I'm telling you!

ANNA—[Turning away in embarrassment.] Quit the kidding, now. [She picks up her bag and goes into the room on left. As soon as she is gone BURKE relapses into an attitude of gloomy thought. CHRIS stares at his beer absent-mindedly. Finally BURKE turns on him.]

BURKE—Is it any religion at all you have, you and your Anna?

CHRIS—[Surprised.] Vhy yes. Ve vas Lutheran in ole country.

BURKE—[Horrified.] Luthers, is it? [Then with a grim resignation, slowly, aloud to himself.] Well, damned then surely. Yerra, what's the difference? 'Tis the will of God, anyway.

84

CHRIS—[Moodily preoccupied with his own thoughts—speaks with somber premonition as ANNA re-enters from the left.] It's funny. It's queer, yes—you and me shipping on same boat dat vay. It ain't right. Ay don't know—it's dat funny vay ole davil sea do her vorst dirty tricks, yes. It's so. [He gets up and goes back and, opening the door, stares out into the darkness.]

BURKE—[Nodding his head in gloomy acquiescence—with a great sigh.] I'm fearing maybe you have the right of it for once, divil take you.

ANNA—[Forcing a laugh.] Gee, Mat, you ain't agreeing with him, are you? [She comes forward and puts her arm about his shoulder—with a determined gaiety.] Aw say, what's the matter? Cut out the gloom. We're all fixed now, ain't we, me and you? [Pours out more beer into his glass and fills one for herself—slaps him on the back.] Come on! Here's to the sea, no matter what! Be a game sport and drink to that! Come on! [She gulps down her glass. Burke banishes his superstitious premonitions with a defiant jerk of his head, grins up at her, and drinks to her toast.]

CHRIS—[Looking out into the night—lost in his somber preoccupation—shakes his head and mutters.] Fog, fog, fog, all bloody time. You can't see vhere you vas going, no. Only dat ole davil, sea—she knows! [The two stare at him. From the harbor comes the muffled, mournful wail of steamers' whistles.]

[The Curtain Falls]

85

"THE FIRST MAN"

A PLAY IN FOUR ACTS

CHARACTERS

CURTIS JAYSON

MARTHA, his wife

JOHN JAYSON, his father, a banker

JOHN, JR., his brother

RICHARD, his brother

ESTHEE (MRS. MARK SHEFFIELD), his sister

LILY, his sister

MRS. DAVIDSON, his father's aunt

MARK SHEFFIELD, a lawyer

EMILY, JOHN JR.'S wife

RICHARD BIGELOW

A MAID

A TRAINED NURSE

TIME—The Present

ACT I

SCENE—Living-room of CURTIS JAYSON'S house in Bridgetown, Conn. A large, comfortable room. On the left, an arm-chair, a big open fireplace, a writing desk with chair in far left corner. On this side there is also a door leading into CURTIS' study. In the rear, center, a double doorway opening on the hall and the entryway. Bookcases are built into the wall on both sides of this doorway. In the far right corner, a grand piano. Three large windows looking out on the lawn, and another arm-chair, front, are on this right side of the room. Opposite the fireplace is a couch, facing front. Opposite the windows on the right is a long table with magazines, reading lamp, etc. Four chairs are grouped about the table. The walls and ceiling are in a French gray color. A great rug covers most of the hardwood floor.

It is around four o'clock of a fine afternoon in early fall.

As the curtain rises, MARTHA, CURTIS and BIGELOW are discovered. MARTHA is a healthy, fine-looking woman of thirty-eight. She does not appear this age for her strenuous life in the open has kept her young and fresh. She possesses the frank, clear, direct quality of outdoors, outspoken and generous. Her wavy hair is a dark brown, her eyes blue-gray. CURTIS JAYSON is a tall, rangy, broad-shouldered man of thirty-seven. While spare, his figure has an appearance of rugged health, of great nervous strength held in reserve. His square-jawed, large-featured face retains an eager boyish enthusiasm in spite of its prevailing expression of thoughtful, preoccupied aloofness. His crisp dark hair is graying at the temples. EDWARD BIGELOW is a large, handsome man of thirty-nine. His face shows culture and tolerance, a sense of humor, a lazy unambitious contentment. CURTIS is reading an article in some scientific periodical, seated by the table. MARTHA and BIGELOW are sitting nearby, laughing and chatting.

BIGELOW—[Is talking with a comically worried but earnest air.] Do you know, I'm getting so I'm actually afraid to leave them alone with that governess. She's too romantic. I'll wager she's got a whole book full of ghost stories, superstitions, and yellow-journal horrors up her sleeve.

MARTHA—Oh, pooh! Don't go milling around for trouble. When I was a kid I used to get fun out of my horrors.

BIGELOW—But I imagine you were more courageous than most of us.

MARTHA—Why?

BIGELOW—Well, Nevada—the Far West at that time—I should think a child would have grown so accustomed to violent scenes—

MARTHA—[Smiling.] Oh, in the mining camps; but you don't suppose my father lugged me along on his prospecting trips, do you? Why, I never saw any rough scenes until I'd finished with school and went to live with father in Goldfield.

BIGELOW—[Smiling.] And then you met Curt.

MARTHA—Yes—but I didn't mean he was a rough scene. He was very mild even in those days. Do tell me what he was like at Cornell.

BIGELOW—A romanticist—and he still is!

MARTHA—[Pointing at CURTIS with gay mischief.] What! That sedate man! Never!

CURTIS—[Looking up and smiling at them both affectionately—lazily.] Don't mind him, Martha. He always was crazy.

88

BIGELOW—[To CURT—accusingly.] Why did you elect to take up mining engineering at Cornell instead of a classical degree at the Yale of your fathers and brothers? Because you had been reading Bret Harte in prep. school and mistaken him for a modern realist. You devoted four years to grooming yourself for another outcast of Poker Flat. [MARTHA laughs.]

CURTIS—[Grinning.] It was you who were hypnotized by Harte—so much so that his West of the past is still your blinded New England-movie idea of the West at present. But go on. What next?

BIGELOW—Next? You get a job as engineer in that Goldfield mine—but you are soon disillusioned by a laborious life where six-shooters are as rare as nuggets. You try prospecting. You find nothing but different varieties of pebbles. But it is necessary to your nature to project romance into these stones, so you go in strong for geology. As a geologist, you become a slave to the Romance of the Rocks. It is but a step from that to anthropology—the last romance of all. There you find yourself—because there is no further to go. You win fame as the most proficient of young skull-hunters—and wander over the face of the globe, digging up bones like an old dog.

CURTIS—[With a laugh.] The man is mad, Martha.

BIGELOW—Mad! What an accusation to come from one who is even now considering setting forth on a five-year excavating contest in search of the remains of our gibbering ancestor, the First Man!

CURTIS—[With sudden seriousness.] I'm not considering it any longer. I've decided to go.

MARTHA—[Starting—the hurt showing in her voice.] When did you decide?

CURTIS—I only really came to a decision this morning. [With a seriousness that forces BIGELOW'S interested attention.] It's a case of got to go. It's a tremendous opportunity that it would be a crime for me to neglect.

BIGELOW—And a big honor, too, isn't it, to be picked as a member of such a large affair?

CURTIS—[With a smile.] I guess it's just that they want all the men with considerable practical experience they can get. There are bound to be hardships and they know I'm hardened to them. [Turning to his wife with an affectionate smile.] We haven't roughed it in the queer corners for the last ten years without knowing how it's done, have we, Martha?

MARTHA—[Dully.] No, Curt.

CURTIS—[With an earnest enthusiasm.] And this expedition IS what you call a large affair, Big. It's the largest thing of its kind ever undertaken. The possibilities, from the standpoint of anthropology, are limitless.

BIGELOW—[With a grin.] Aha! Now we come to the Missing Link!

CURTIS—[Frowning.] Darn your Barnum and Bailey circus lingo, Big. This isn't a thing to mock at. I should think the origin of man would be something that would appeal even to your hothouse imagination. Modern science believes—knows—that Asia was the first home of the human race. That's where we're going, to the great Central Asian plateau north of the Himalayas.

BIGELOW—[More soberly.] And there you hope to dig up—our first ancestor?

CURTIS—It's a chance in a million, but I believe we may, myself— at least find authentic traces of him so that we can reconstruct his life and habits. I was up in that country a lot while I was mining advisor to the Chinese government—did some of my own work on the side. The extraordinary results I obtained with the little means at my disposal convinced me of the riches yet to be uncovered. The First Man may be among them.

BIGELOW—[Turning to MARTHA.] And you were with him on that Asian plateau?

MARTHA—Yes, I've always been with him.

CURTIS—You bet she has. [He goes over and puts his hand on his wife's shoulder affectionately.] Martha's more efficient than a whole staff of assistants and secretaries. She knows more about what I'm doing than I do half the time. [He turns toward his study.] Well, I guess I'll go in and work some.

MARTHA—[Quietly.] Do you need me now, Curt?

BIGELOW—[Starting up.] Yes, if you two want to work together, why just shoo me—

CURTIS—[Puts both hands on his shoulders and forces him to his seat again.] No. Sit down, Big. I don't need Martha now. [Coming over to her, bends down and kisses her—rather mockingly.] I couldn't deprive Big of an audience for his confessions of a fond parent.

BIGELOW—Aha! Now it's you who are mocking at something you know nothing about. [An awkward silence follows this remark.]

CURTIS—[Frowning.] I guess you're forgetting, aren't you, Big? [He turns and walks into his study, closing the door gently behind him.]

MARTHA—[After a pause—sadly.] Poor Curt.

BIGELOW—[Ashamed and confused.] I had forgotten—

MARTHA—The years have made me reconciled. They haven't Curt. [She sighs—then turns to BIGELOW with a forced smile.] I suppose it's hard for any of you back here to realize that Curt and I ever had any children.

BIGELOW—[After a pause.] How old were they when—?

MARTHA—Three years and two—both girls. [She goes on sadly.] We had a nice little house in Goldfield. [Forcing a smile.] We were very respectable home folks then. The wandering came later,

91

after—It was a Sunday in winter when Curt and I had gone visiting some friends. The nurse girl fell asleep—or something—and the children sneaked out in their underclothes and played in the snow. Pneumonia set in—and a week later they were both dead.

BIGELOW—[Shocked.] Good heavens!

MARTHA—We were real lunatics for a time. And then when we'd calmed down enough to realize—how things stood with us—we swore we'd never have children again—to steal away their memory. It wasn't what you thought—romanticism—that set Curt wandering—and me with him. It was a longing to lose ourselves—to forget. He flung himself with all his power into every new study that interested him. He couldn't keep still, mentally or bodily—and I followed. He needed me—then—so dreadfully!

BIGELOW—And is it that keeps driving him on now?

MARTHA—Oh, no. He's found himself. His work has taken the place of the children.

BIGELOW—And with you, too?

MARTHA—[With a wan smile.] Well, I've helped—all I could. His work has me in it, I like to think—and I have him.

BIGELOW—[Shaking his head.] I think people are foolish to stand by such an oath as you took—forever. [With a smile.] Children are a great comfort in one's old age, I've tritely found.

MARTHA—[Smiling.] Old age!

BIGELOW—I'm knocking at the door of fatal forty.

MARTHA—[With forced gaiety.] You're not very tactful, I must say. Don't you know I'm thirty-eight?

BIGELOW—[Gallantly.] A woman is as old as she looks. You're not thirty yet.

92

MARTHA—[Laughing.] After that nice remark I'll have to forgive you everything, won't I? [LILY JAYSON comes in from the rear. She is a slender, rather pretty girl of twenty-five. The stamp of college student is still very much about her. She rather insists on a superior, intellectual air, is full of nervous, thwarted energy. At the sight of them sitting on the couch together, her eyebrows are raised.]

LILY—[Coming into the room—breezily.] Hello, Martha. Hello, Big. [They both get up with answering "Hellos."] I walked right in regardless. Hope I'm not interrupting.

MARTHA—Not at all.

LILY—[Sitting down by the table as MARTHA and BIGELOW resume their seats on the lounge.] I must say it sounded serious. I heard you tell Big you'd forgive him everything, Martha. [Dryly—with a mocking glance at BIGELOW.] You're letting yourself in for a large proposition.

BIGELOW—[Displeased but trying to smile it off.] The past is never past for a dog with a bad name, eh, Lily? [LILY laughs. BIGELOW gets up.] If you want to reward me for my truthfulness, Mrs. Jayson, help me take the kids for an airing in the car. I know it's an imposition but they've grown to expect you. [Glancing at his watch.] By Jove, I'll have to run along. I'll get them and then pick you up here. Is that all right?

MARTHA—Fine.

BIGELOW—I'll run, then. Good-by, Lily. [She nods. BIGELOW goes out rear.]

MARTHA—[Cordially.] Come on over here, Lily.

LILY—[Sits on couch with MARTHA—after a pause—with a smile.] You were forgetting, weren't you?

MARTHA—What?

93

LILY—That you'd invited all the family over here to tea this afternoon. I'm the advance guard.

MARTHA—[Embarrassed.] So I was! How stupid!

LILY—[With an inquisitive glance at MARTHA'S face but with studied carelessness.] Do you like Bigelow?

MARTHA—Yes, very much. And Curt thinks the world of him.

LILY—Oh, Curt is the last one to be bothered by anyone's morals. Curt and I are the unconventional ones of the family. The trouble with Bigelow, Martha, is that he was too careless to conceal his sins—and that won't go down in this Philistine small town. You have to hide and be a fellow hypocrite or they revenge themselves on you. Bigelow didn't. He flaunted his love-affairs in everyone's face. I used to admire him for it. No one exactly blamed him, in their secret hearts. His wife was a terrible, straitlaced creature. No man could have endured her. [Disgustedly.] After her death he suddenly acquired a bad conscience. He'd never noticed the children before. I'll bet he didn't even know their names. And then, presto, he's about in our midst giving an imitation of a wet hen with a brood of ducks. It's a bore, if you ask me.

MARTHA—[Flushing.] I think it's very fine of him.

LILY—[Shaking her head.] His reform is too sudden. He's joined the hypocrites, I think.

MARTHA—I'm sure he's no hypocrite. When you see him with the children—

LILY—Oh, I know he's a good actor. Lots of women have been in love with him. [Then suddenly.] You won't be furious if I'm very, very frank, will you, Martha?

MARTHA—[Surprised.] No, of course not, Lily.

LILY—Well, I'm the bearer of a message from the Jayson family.

94

MARTHA—[Astonished.] A message? For me?

LILY—Don't think that I have anything to do with it. I'm only a Victor record of their misgivings. Shall I switch it going? Well, then, father thinks, brother John and wife, sister Esther and husband all think that you are unwisely intimate with this same Bigelow.

MARTHA—[Stunned.] I? Unwisely intimate—? [Suddenly laughing with amusement.] Well, you sure are funny people!

LILY—No, we're not funny. We'd be all right if we were. On the contrary, we're very dull and deadly. Bigelow really has a villainous rep. for philandering. But, of course, you didn't know that.

MARTHA—[Beginning to feel resentful—coldly.] No, I didn't—and I don't care to know it now.

LILY—[Calmly.] I told them you wouldn't relish their silly advice. [In a very confidential, friendly tone.] Oh, I hate their narrow small-town ethics as much as you do, Martha. I sympathize with you, indeed I do. But I have to live with them and so, for comfort's sake, I've had to make compromises. And you're going to live in our midst from now on, aren't you? Well then, you'll have to make compromises, too—if you want any peace.

MARTHA—But-compromises about what? [Forcing a laugh.] I refuse to take it seriously. How anyone could think—it's too absurd.

LILY—What set them going was Big's being around such an awful lot the weeks Curt was in New York, just after you'd settled down here. You must acknowledge he was-very much present then, Martha.

MARTHA—But it was on account of his children. They were always with him.

LILY—The town doesn't trust this sudden fond parenthood, Martha. We've known him too long, you see.

MARTHA—But he's Curt's oldest and best friend.

LILY—We've found they always are.

MARTHA—[Springing to her feet—indignantly.] It's a case of evil minds, it seems to me—and it would be extremely insulting if I didn't have a sense of humor. [Resentfully.] You can tell your family, that as far as I'm concerned, the town may—

LILY—Go to the devil. I knew you'd say that. Well, fight the good fight. You have all my best wishes. [With a sigh.] I wish I had something worth fighting for. Now that I'm through with college, my occupation's gone. All I do is read book after book. The only live people are the ones in books, I find, and the only live life.

MARTHA—[Immediately sympathetic.] You're lonely, that's what, Lily.

LILY—[Drily.] Don't pity me, Martha—or I'll join the enemy.

MARTHA—I'm not. But I'd like to help you if I could. [After a pause.] Have you ever thought of marrying?

LILY—[With a laugh.] Martha! How banal! The men I see are enough to banish that thought if I ever had it.

MARTHA—Marriage isn't only the man. It's children. Wouldn't you like to have children?

LILY—[Turning to her bluntly.] Wouldn't you?

MARTHA—[Confused.] But—Lily—

LILY—Oh, I know it wasn't practicable as long as you elected to wander with Curt—but why not now when you've definitely settled down here? I think that would solve things all round. If you could present Father with a grandson, I'm sure he'd fall on your neck. He feels piqued at the John and Esther families because they've had a run of girls. A male Jayson! Aunt Davidson would weep with joy. [Suddenly.] You're thirty-eight, aren't you, Martha?

96

MARTHA—Yes. LILY—Then why don't you—before it's too late? [MARTHA, struggling with herself, does not answer. LILY goes on slowly.] You won't want to tag along with Curt to the ends of the earth forever, will you? [Curiously.] Wasn't that queer life like any other? I mean, didn't it get to pall on you?

MARTHA—[As if confessing it reluctantly.] Yes—perhaps—in the last two years.

LILY—[Decisively.] It's time for both of you to rest on your laurels. Why can't Curt keep on with what he's doing now—stay home and write his books?

MARTHA—Curt isn't that kind. The actual work—the romance of it—that's his life.

LILY—But if he goes and you have to stay, you'll be lonesome—[meaningly] alone.

MARTHA—Horribly. I don't know what I'll do.

LILY—Then why—why? Think, Martha. If Curt knew—that was to happen—he'd want to stay here with you. I'm sure he would.

MARTHA—[Shaking her head sadly.] No. Curt has grown to dislike children. They remind him of—ours that were taken. He adored them so—he's never become reconciled.

LILY—If you confronted Curt with the actual fact, he'd be reconciled soon enough, and happy in the bargain.

MARTHA—[Eagerly.] Do you really think so?

LILY—And you, Martha—I can tell from the way you've talked that you'd like to.

MARTHA—[Excitedly.] Yes, I—I never thought I'd ever want to again. For many years after they died I never once dreamed of it— But lately—the last years—I've felt—and when we came to live here—and I saw all around me—homes—and children, I—[She hesitates as if ashamed at having confessed so much.]

LILY—[Putting an arm around her—affectionately.] I know. [Vigorously.] You must, that's all there is to it! If you want my advice, you go right ahead and don't tell Curt until it's a fact he'll have to learn to like, willy-nilly. You'll find, in his inmost heart, he'll be tickled to death.

MARTHA—[Forcing a smile.] Yes, I—I'll confess I thought of that. In spite of my fear, I—I've—I mean—I—[She flushes in a shamed confusion.]

LILY—[Looking at her searchingly.] Why, Martha, what—[Then suddenly understanding—with excited pleasure.] Martha! I know! It is so, isn't it? It is!

MARTHA—[In a whisper.] Yes.

LILY—[Kissing her affectionately.] You dear, you! [Then after a pause.] How long have you known?

MARTHA—For over two months. [There is a ring from the front door bell in the hall.]

LILY—[Jumping up.] I'll bet that's we Jaysons now. [She runs to the door in the rear and looks down the hall to the right.] Yes, it's Esther and husband and Aunt Davidson. [She comes back to MARTHA laughing excitedly. The MAID is seen going to the door.] The first wave of attack, Martha! Be brave! The Young Guard dies but never surrenders!

MARTHA—[Displeased but forcing a smile.] You make me feel terribly ill at ease when you put it that way, Lily. [She rises now and goes to greet the visitors, who enter. MRS. DAVIDSON is seventy-five years old—a thin, sinewy old lady, old-fashioned, unbending and rigorous in manner. She is dressed aggressively in the fashion of a bygone age. ESTHER is a stout, middle-aged woman with the round, unmarked, sentimentally—contented face of one who lives unthinkingly from day to day, sheltered in an assured position in her little world. MARK, her husband, is a lean, tall, stooping man of about forty-five. His long face is alert, shrewd, cautious, full of the superficial craftiness of the lawyer mind. MARTHA kisses the two women, shakes hands with MARK, uttering the usual meaningless greetings in a forced tone. They reply in much the same spirit. There is the buzz of this empty chatter while MARTHA gets them seated. LILY stands looking on with a cynical smile of amusement. MRS. DAVIDSON is in the chair at the end of table, left, ESTHER sits by MARTHA on couch, MARK in chair at front of table.] Will you have tea now or shall we wait for the others?

ESTHER—Let's wait. They ought to be here any moment.

LILY—[Maliciously.] Just think, Martha had forgotten you were coming. She was going motoring with Bigelow. [There is a dead silence at this—broken diplomatically by SHEFFIELD.]

SHEFFIELD—Where is Curt, Martha?

MARTHA—Hard at work in his study. I'm afraid he's there for the day. SHEFFIELD—[Condescendingly.] Still plugging away at his book, I suppose. Well, I hope it will be a big success.

LILY—[Irritated by his smugness.] As big a success as the brief you're writing to restrain the citizens from preventing the Traction Company robbing them, eh Mark? [Before anyone can reply, she turns suddenly on her aunt who is sitting rigidly on her chair, staring before her stonily like some old lady in a daguerreotype—in a loud challenging tone.] You don't mind if I smoke, Aunt? [She takes a cigarette out of case and lights it.]

ESTHER—[Smiling.] Lily!

MRS. DAVIDSON—[Fixes LILY with her stare—in a tone of irrevocable decision.] We'll get you married, young lady, and that very soon. What you need to bring you down to earth is a husband and the responsibility of children. [Turning her glance to MARTHA, a challenge in her question.] Every woman who is able should have children. Don't you believe that, Martha Jayson? [She accentuates the full name.]

99

MARTHA—[Taken aback for a moment but restraining her resentment—gently.] Yes, I do, Mrs. Davidson.

MRS. DAVIDSON—[Seemingly placated by this reply—in a milder tone.] You must call me aunt, my dear. [Meaningly.] All the Jaysons do.

MARTHA—[Simply.] Thank you, aunt.

LILY—[As if all of this aroused her irritation—in a nervous fuming.] Why don't the others come, darn 'em? I'm dying for my tea. [The door from the study is opened and CURT appears. They all greet him.]

CURTIS—[Absent-mindedly.] Hello, everybody. [Then with a preoccupied air to MARTHA.] Martha, I don't want to interrupt you—but—

MARTHA—[Getting up briskly.] You want my help?

CURTIS—[With the same absent-minded air.] Yes—not for long—just a few notes before I forget them. [He goes back into the study.]

MARTHA—[Seemingly relieved by this interruption and glad of the chance it gives to show them her importance to CURT.] You'll excuse me for a few moments, all of you, won't you? [They all nod.]

MRS. DAVIDSON—[Rather harshly.] Why doesn't Curt hire a secretary? That is no work for his wife.

MARTHA—[Quietly.] A paid secretary could hardly give the sympathy and understanding Curt needs, Mrs. Davidson. [Proudly.] And she would have to study for years, as I have done, in order to take my place. [To LILY.] If I am not here by the time the others arrive, will you see about the tea, Lily—?

LILY—[Eagerly.] Sure. I love to serve drinks. If I were a man, I'd be a bartender—in Mexico or Canada.

MARTHA—[Going toward the study.] I'll be with you again in a minute, I hope. [She goes in and shuts the door behind her.]

ESTHER—[Pettishly.] Even people touched by a smattering of science seem to get rude, don't they?

MRS. DAVIDSON—[Harshly.] I have heard much silly talk of this being an age of free women, and I have always said it was tommyrot. [Pointing to the study.] She is an example. She is more of a slave to Curt's hobbies than any of my generation were to anything but their children. [Still more harshly.] Where are her children?

LILY—They died, Aunt, as children have a bad habit of doing. [Then meaningly.] However, I wouldn't despair if I were you. [MRS. DAVIDSON stares at her fixedly.]

ESTHER—[Betraying a sudden frightened jealousy.] What do you mean, Lily? What are you so mysterious about? What did she say? What—?

LILY—[Mockingly.] Mark, your frau seems to have me on the stand. Can I refuse to answer? [There is a ring at the bell. LILY jumps to her feet excitedly.] Here comes the rest of our Grand Fleet. Now I'll have my tea. [She darts out to the hallway.]

ESTHER—[Shaking her head.] Goodness, Lily is trying on the nerves. [JAYSON, his two sons, JOHN and DICK, and JOHN's wife, EMILY, enter from hallway in rear. JAYSON, the father, is a short, stout, bald-headed man of sixty. A typical, small-town, New England best-family banker, reserved in pose, unobtrusively important—a placid exterior hiding querulousness and a fussy temper. JOHN JUNIOR is his father over again in appearance, but pompous, obtrusive, purse-and-family-proud, extremely irritating in his self-complacent air of authority, emptily assertive and loud. He is about forty. RICHARD, the other brother, is a typical young Casino and country club member, college-bred, good looking, not unlikable. He has been an officer in the war and has not forgotten it. EMILY, JOHN JR.'s wife, is one of those small, mouse-like women who conceal beneath an outward aspect of gentle, unprotected innocence a very active envy, a silly pride, and a mean malice. The

101

people in the room with the exception of MRS. DAVIDSON rise to greet them. All exchange familiar, perfunctory greetings. SHEFFIELD relinquishes his seat in front of the table to JAYSON, going to the chair, right front, himself. JOHN and DICK take the two chairs to the rear of table. EMILY joins ESTHER on the couch and they whisper together excitedly, ESTHER doing most of the talking. The men remain in uncomfortable silence for a moment.]

DICK—[With gay mockery.] Well, the gang's all here. Looks like the League of Nations. [Then with impatience.] Let's get down to cases, folks. I want to know why I've been summoned here. I'm due for tournament mixed-doubles at the Casino at five. Where's the tea—and has Curt a stick in the cellar to put in it?

LILY—[Appearing in the doorway.] Here's tea—but no stick for you, sot. [The MAID brings in tray with tea things.]

JOHN—[Heavily.] It seems it would be more to the point to inquire where our hostess—

JAYSON—[Rousing himself again.] Yes. And where is Curt?

LILY—Working at his book. He called Martha to take notes on something.

ESTHER—[With a trace of resentment.] She left us as if she were glad of the excuse.

LILY—Stuff, Esther! She knows how much Curt depends on her—and we don't.

EMILY—[In her quiet, lisping voice—with the most innocent air.] Martha seems to be a model wife. [But there is some quality to the way she says it that makes them all stare at her uneasily.]

LILY—[Insultingly.] How well you say what you don't mean, Emily! Twinkle, twinkle, little bat! But I'm forgetting to do the honors. Tea, everybody? [Without waiting for any answer.] Tea, everybody! [The tea is served.]

102

JAYSON—[Impatiently.] Stop fooling, Lily. Let's get to our muttons. Did you talk with Martha?

LILY—[Briskly.] I did, sir.

JAYSON—[In a lowered voice.] What did she say?

LILY—She said you could all go to the devil! [They all look shocked and insulted. LILY enjoys this, then adds quietly.] Oh, not in those words. Martha is a perfect lady. But she made it plain she will thank you to mind your own business.

ESTHER—[Volubly.] And just imagine, she'd even forgotten she'd asked us here this afternoon and was going motoring with Bigelow.

LILY—With his three children, too, don't forget.

EMILY—[Softly.] They have become such well-behaved and intelligent children, they say. [Again all the others hesitate, staring at her suspiciously.]

LILY—[Sharply.] You'd better let Martha train yours for a while, Emily. I'm sure she'd improve their manners—though, of course, she couldn't give them any intelligence.

EMILY—[With the pathos of outraged innocence.] Oh!

DICK—[Interrupting.] So it's Bigelow you're up in the air about? [He gives a low whistle—then frowns angrily.] The deuce you say!

LILY—[Mockingly.] Look at our soldier boy home from the wars getting serious about the family honor! It's too bad this is a rough, untutored country where they don't permit dueling, isn't it, Dick?

DICK—[His pose crumbling—angrily.] Go to the devil!

SHEFFIELD—[With a calm, judicious air.] This wrangling is getting us nowhere. You say she was resentful about our well-meant word to the wise? JAYSON—[Testily.] Surely she must realize that some consideration is due the position she occupies in Bridgetown as Curt's wife.

103

LILY—Martha is properly unimpressed by big frogs in tiny puddles. And there you are.

MRS. DAVIDSON—[Outraged.] The idea! She takes a lot upon herself—the daughter of a Wild Western coal-miner.

LILY—[Mockingly.] Gold miner, Aunt.

MRS. DAVIDSON—It makes no difference—a common miner! SHEFFIELD— [Keenly inquisitive.] Just before the others came, Lily, you gave out some hints—very definite hints, I should say—

ESTHER—[Excitedly.] Yes, you did, Lily. What did you mean?

LILY—[Uncertainly.] Perhaps I shouldn't have. It's not my secret. [Enjoying herself immensely now that she holds the spotlight—after a pause, in a stage whisper.] Shall I tell you? Yes, I can't help telling. Well, Martha is going to have a son. [They are all stunned and flabbergasted and stare at her speechlessly.]

MRS. DAVIDSON—[Her face lighting up—joyously.] A son! Curt's son!

JAYSON—[Pleased by the idea but bewildered.] A son?

DICK—[Smartly.] Lily's kidding you. How can she know it's a son—unless she's a clairvoyant.

ESTHER—[With glad relief.] Yes, how stupid!

LILY—I am clairvoyant in this case. Allah is great and it will be a son—if only to make you and Emily burst with envy among your daughters.

ESTHER—Lily!

EMILY—Oh!

JAYSON—[Testily.] Keep still for a moment, Lily, for God's sake. This is no subject to joke about, remember.

LILY—Martha told me. I know that.

JAYSON—And does Curt know this?

LILY—No, not yet. Martha has been afraid to tell him.

JAYSON—Ah, that explains matters. You know I asked Curt some time ago—and he said it was impossible.

EMILY—[With a lift of her eyebrows.] Impossible? Why, what a funny thing to say.

SHEFFIELD—[Keenly lawyer-like.] And why is Martha afraid to tell him, Lily?

LILY—It's all very simple. When the two died years ago, they said they would never have one again. Martha thinks Curt is still haunted by their memory and is afraid he will resent another as an intruder. I told her that was all foolishness—that a child was the one thing to make Curt settle down for good at home here and write his books.

JAYSON—[Eagerly.] Yes, I believe that myself. [Pleased.] Well, this is fine news.

EMILY—Still it was her duty to tell Curt, don't you think? I don't see how she could be afraid of Curt—for those reasons. [They all stare at her.]

ESTHER—[Resentfully.] I don't, either. Why, Curt's the biggest-hearted and kindest—

EMILY—I wonder how long she's known—this?

LILY—[Sharply.] Two months, she said.

EMILY—Two months? [She lets this sink in.]

JOHN—[Quickly scenting something—eagerly.] What do you mean, Emily? [Then as if he read her mind.] Two months? But before that—Curt was away in New York almost a month!

105

LILY—[Turning on EMILY fiercely.] So! You got someone to say it for you as you always do, Poison Mind! Oh, I wish the ducking stool had never been abolished!

EMILY—[Growing crimson—falteringly.] I—I didn't mean—

JOHN—[Furiously.] Where the honor of the family is at stake—

LILY—[Fiercely.] Ssshh, you empty barrel! I think I hear— [The door from the study is opened and MARTHA comes in in the midst of a heavy silence. All the gentlemen rise stiffly. MARTHA is made immediately self-conscious and resentful by the feeling that they have been discussing her unfavorably.]

MARTHA—[Coming forward—with a forced cordiality.] How do you do, everybody? So sorry I wasn't here when you came. I hope Lily made proper excuses for me. [She goes from one to the other of the four latest comers with "So glad you came," etc. They reply formally and perfunctorily. MARTHA finally finds a seat on the couch between EMILY and ESTHER.] I hope Lily—but I see you've all had tea.

LILY—[Trying to save the situation—gayly.] Yes. You can trust me as understudy for the part of hostess any time.

MARTHA—[Forcing a smile.] Well, I'm glad to know I wasn't missed.

EMILY—[Sweetly.] We were talking about you—at least, we were listening to Lily talk about you.

MARTHA—[Stiffening defensively.] About me?

EMILY—Yes—about how devoted you were to Curt's work. [LILY gives her a venomous glance of scorn.]

MARTHA—[Pleased but inwardly uneasy.] Oh, but you see I consider it my work, too, I've helped him with it so long now.

JAYSON—[In a forced tone.] And how is Curt's book coming, Martha?

106

MARTHA—[More and more stung by their strained attitudes and inquisitive glances. Coldly and cuttingly.] Finely, thank you. The book will cause quite a stir, I believe. It will make the name of Jayson famous in the big world outside of Bridgetown.

MRS. DAVIDSON—[Indignantly.] The name of Jayson has been—

JAYSON—[Pleadingly.] Aunt Elizabeth!

LILY—Aunt means it's world famous already, Martha. [Pointing to the sullen JOHN.] John was once a substitute on the Yale Freshman soccer team, you know. If it wasn't for his weak shins he would have made the team, fancy!

DICK—[This tickles his sense of humor and he bursts into laughter.] Lily wins! [As his brother glares at him—looking at his watch.] Heavens, I'll have to hustle! [Gets to his feet.] I'm due at the Casino. [Comes and shakes MARTHA's hand formally.] I'm sorry I can't stay.

MARTHA—So glad you came. Do come in again any time. We keep open house, you know—Western fashion. [She accentuates this.]

DICK—[Hurriedly.] Delighted to. [He starts for the door in rear.]

LILY—[As if suddenly making up her mind.] Wait a second! I'm coming with you—

DICK—Sure thing—only hurry, darn you! [He goes out.]

LILY—[Stops at the door in rear and catching MARTHA's eye, looks meaningly at the others.] Phew! I need fresh air! [She makes an encouraging motion as if pummeling someone to MARTHA, indicating her assembled family as the victim—then goes out laughing. A motor is heard starting—running off.]

ESTHER—[With a huge sigh of relief.] Thank goodness, she's gone. What a vixen! What would you do if you had a sister like that, Martha?

107

MARTHA—I'd love her—and try to understand her.

SHEFFIELD—[Meaningly.] She's a bad ally to rely on—this side of the fence one day, and that the next.

MARTHA—Is that why you advised her to become a lawyer, Mr. Sheffield?

SHEFFIELD—[Stung, but maintaining an unruffled front.] Now, now, that remark must be catalogued as catty.

MARTHA—[Defiantly.] It seems to be in the Bridgetown atmosphere. I never was—not the least bit—in the open air.

JAYSON—[Conciliatingly.] Oh, Bridgetown isn't so bad, Martha, once you get used to us.

JOHN—It's one of the most prosperous and wealthy towns in the U.S.—and that means in the world, nowadays.

EMILY—[With her sugary smile.] That isn't what Martha means, you silly. I know what she's thinking about us, and I'm not sure that I don't agree with her—partly. She feels that we're so awfully strict—about certain things. It must be so different in the Far West—I suppose—so much freer.

MARTHA—[Acidly.] Then you believe broad-mindedness and clean thinking are a question of locality? I can't agree with you. I know nothing of the present Far West, not having lived there for ten years, but Curt and I have lived in the Far East and I'm sure he'd agree with me in saying that Chinese ancestor worship is far more dignified than ours. After all, you know, theirs is religion, not snobbery. [There is a loud honking of an auto horn before the house. MARTHA starts, seems to come to a quick decision, and announces with studied carelessness.] That must be Mr. Bigelow. I suppose Lily told you I had an engagement to go motoring with him. So sorry I must leave. But I'm like Lily. I need fresh air. [She walks to the study door as she is talking.] I'll call Curt. [She raps loudly on the door and calls.] Curt! Come out! It's important. [She turns and goes to the door, smiling fixedly.] He'll be out when he's through swearing. [She goes out, rear.]

JOHN—[Exploding.] Well, of all the damned cheek!

ESTHER—She shows her breeding, I must say.

EMILY—[With horror.] Oh, how rude—and insulting.

MRS. DAVIDSON—[Rising rigidly to her feet.] I will never set foot in this house again! JAYSON—[Jumping up to restrain her—worriedly.] Now, Aunt Elizabeth, do keep your head! We must have no scandal of any sort. Remember there are servants about. Do sit down. [The old lady refuses in stubborn silence.]

SHEFFIELD—[Judiciously.] One must make allowances for one in her condition, Aunt.

JAYSON—[Snatching at this.] Exactly. Remember her condition. Aunt [testily] and do sit down. [The old lady plumps herself down again angrily.]

EMILY—[In her lisp of hidden meanings.] Yes, the family mustn't forget—her condition. [The door from the study is opened and CURT appears. His face shows his annoyance at being interrupted, his eyes are preoccupied. They all turn and greet him embarrassedly. He nods silently and comes slowly down front.]

CURTIS—[Looking around.] Where's Martha? What's the important thing she called me out for?

ESTHER—[Forcing gaiety.] To play host, you big bear, you! Don't you think we came to see you, too? Sit down here and be good. [He sits on sofa.]

EMILY—[Softly.] Martha had to leave us to go motoring with Mr. Bigelow.

ESTHER—[Hastily.] And the three children.

CURTIS—[Frowning grumpily.] Hm! Big and his eternal kids. [He sighs. They exchange meaning glances. CURT seems to feel ashamed of his grumpiness and tries to fling it off—with a cheerful smile.] But what the deuce! I must be getting selfish to grudge Martha her bit of fresh air. You don't know what it means to outdoor animals like us to be pent up. [He springs to his feet and paces back and forth nervously.] We're used to living with the sky for a roof—[Then interestedly.] Did Martha tell you I'd definitely decided to go on the five year Asian expedition?

ESTHER—Curt! You're not!

EMILY—And leave Martha here—all alone—for five years?

JAYSON—Yes, you can't take Martha with you this time, you know.

CURTIS—[With a laugh.] No? What makes you so sure of that? [As they look mystified, he continues confidentially.] I'll let you in on the secret—only you must all promise not to breathe a word to Martha—until to-morrow. To-morrow is her birthday, you know, and this is a surprise I've saved for her. [They all nod.] I've been intriguing my damnedest for the past month to get permission for Martha to go with me. It was difficult because women are supposed to be barred. [Happily.] But I've succeeded. The letter came this morning. How tickled to death she'll be when she hears! I know she's given up hope. [Thoughtfully.] I suppose it's that has been making her act so out-of-sorts lately.

JAYSON—[Worriedly.] Hmm! But would you persist in going—alone—if you knew it was impossible for her—?

CURTIS—[Frowning.] I can't imagine it without her. You people can't have any idea what a help—a chum—she's been. You can't believe that a woman could be—so much that—in a life of that kind—how I've grown to depend on her. The thousand details—she attends to them all. She remembers everything. Why, I'd be lost. I wouldn't know how to start. [With a laugh.] I know this sounds like a confession of weakness but it's true just the same. [Frowning

110

again.] However, naturally my work must always be the first consideration. Yes, absolutely! [Then with glad relief.] But what's the use of rambling on this way? We can both go, thank heaven!

MRS. DAVIDSON—[Sternly.] No. SHE cannot go. And it is YOUR duty—

CURTIS—[Interrupting her with a trace of impatience.] Oh, come! That's all nonsense, Aunt. You don't understand the kind of woman Martha is.

MRS. DAVIDSON—[Harshly.] The women I understand prefer rearing their children to selfish gallivanting over the world.

CURTIS—[Impatiently.] But we have no children now, Aunt.

MRS. DAVIDSON—I know that, more's the pity. But later—

CURTIS—[Emphatically.] No, I tell you! It's impossible!

MRS. DAVIDSON—[Grimly.] I have said my last word. Go your own road and work your own ruin.

CURTIS—[Brusquely.] I think I'll change my togs and go for a walk. Excuse me for a second. I'll be right down again. [He goes out, rear.]

EMILY—[With her false air of innocence.] Curt acts so funny, doesn't he? Did you notice how emphatic he was about its being impossible? And he said Martha seemed to him to be acting queer lately—with him, I suppose he meant.

ESTHER—He certainly appeared put out when he heard she'd gone motoring with Big.

JAYSON—[Moodily.] This dislike of the very mention of children. It isn't like Curt, not a bit.

JOHN—There's something rotten in Denmark somewhere. This family will yet live to regret having accepted a stranger—

SHEFFIELD—[Mollifyingly—with a judicial air.] Come now! This is

111

all only suspicion. There is no evidence; you have no case; and the defendant is innocent until you have proved her guilty, remember. [Getting to his feet.] Well, let's break up. Esther, you and I ought to be getting home. [They all rise.]

JAYSON—[Testily.] Well, if I were sure it would all blow over without any open scandal, I'd offer up a prayer of thanks. [The Curtain Falls]

112

ACT II

SCENE—CURTIS JAYSON'S study. On the left, forward, a gun rack in which are displayed several varieties of rifles and shotguns. Farther back, three windows looking out on the garden. In the rear wall, an open fireplace with two leather arm-chairs in front of it. To right of fireplace, a door leading into the living-room. In the far right corner, another chair. In the right wall, three windows looking out on the lawn and garden. On this side, front, a typewriting table with machine and chair. Opposite the windows on the right, a bulky leather couch, facing front. In front of the windows on the left, a long table with stacks of paper piled here and there on it, reference books, etc. On the left of table, a swivel chair. Gray oak bookcases are built into the cream rough plaster walls which are otherwise almost hidden from view by a collection of all sorts of hunter's trophies, animal heads of all kinds. The floor is covered with animal skins—tiger, polar bear, leopard, lion, etc. Skins are also thrown over the backs of the chairs. The sections of the bookcase not occupied by scientific volumes have been turned into a specimen case for all sorts of zoological, geological, anthropological oddities.

It is mid-morning, sunny and bright, of the following day.

CURTIS and BIGELOW are discovered. CURTIS is half-sitting on the corner of the table, left, smoking a pipe. BIGELOW is lying sprawled on the couch. Through the open windows on the right come the shouts of children playing. MARTHA's voice joins in with theirs.

BIGELOW—Listen to that rumpus, will you! The kids are having the time of their lives. [He goes to the window and looks out—

delightedly.] Your wife is playing hide and seek with them. Come and look.

CURTIS—[With a trace of annoyance.] Oh, I can see well enough from here.

BIGELOW—[With a laugh.] She seems to get as much fun out of it as they do. [As a shriek comes from outside—excitedly.] Ah, Eddy discovered her behind the tree. Isn't he tickled now! [He turns back from the window and lights a cigarette—enthusiastically.] Jove, what a hand she is with children!

CURTIS—[As if the subject bored him.] Oh, Martha gets along well with anyone.

BIGELOW—[Sits on the couch again—with a sceptical smile.] You think so? With everyone?

CURTIS—[Surprised.] Yes—with everyone we've ever come in contact with—even aboriginal natives.

BIGELOW—With the aboriginal natives of Bridgetown? With the well-known Jayson family, for example?

CURTIS—[Getting to his feet—frowning.] Why, everything's all right between Martha and them, isn't it? What do you mean, Big? I certainly imagined—but I'll confess this damn book has had me so preoccupied—

BIGELOW—Too darn preoccupied, if you'll pardon my saying so. It's not fair to leave her to fight it alone.

CURTIS—[Impatiently.] Fight what? Martha has a sense of humor. I'm sure their petty prejudices merely amuse her.

BIGELOW—[Sententiously.] A mosquito is a ridiculous, amusing creature, seen under a microscope; but when a swarm has been stinging you all night—

CURTIS—[A broad grin coming over his face.] You speak from experience, eh?

BIGELOW—[Smiling.] You bet I do. Touch me anywhere and you'll find a bite. This, my native town, did me the honor of devoting its entire leisure attention for years to stinging me to death.

CURTIS—Well, if I am to believe one-tenth of the family letters I used to receive on the subject of my old friend, Bigelow, they sure had just cause.

BIGELOW—Oh, I'll play fair. I'll admit they did—then. But it's exasperating to know they never give you credit for changing—I almost said, reforming, One ought to be above the gossip of a town like this—but say what you like, it does get under your skin.

CURTIS—[With an indulgent smile.] So you'd like to be known as a reformed character, eh?

BIGELOW—[Rather ruefully.] Et tu! Your tone is sceptical. But I swear to you, Curt, I'm an absolutely new man since my wife's death, since I've grown to love the children. Before that I hardly knew them. They were hers, not mine, it seemed. [His face lighting up.] Now we're the best of pals, and I've commenced to appreciate life from a different angle. I've found a career at last—the children—the finest career a man could have, I believe.

CURTIS—[Indifferently.] Yes, I suppose so—if you're made that way.

BIGELOW—Meaning you're not?

CURTIS—Not any more. [Frowning.] I tried that once.

BIGELOW—[After a pause—with a smile.] But we're wandering from the subject of Martha versus the mosquitoes.

CURTIS—[With a short laugh.] Oh, to the deuce with that! Trust Martha to take care of herself. Besides, I'll have her out of this stagnant hole before so very long—six months, to be exact.

BIGELOW—Where do you think of settling her then?

115

CURTIS—No settling about it. I'm going to take her with me.

BIGELOW—[Surprised.] On the Asian expedition?

CURTIS—Yes. I haven't told her yet but I'm going to to-day. It's her birthday—and I've been saving the news to surprise her with.

BIGELOW—Her birthday? I wish the children and I had known—but it's not too late yet.

CURTIS—[With a grin.] Thirty-nine candles, if you're thinking of baking a cake!

BIGELOW—[Meaningly.] That's not old—but it's not young either, Curt.

CURTIS—[Disgustedly.] You talk like an old woman, Big. What have years to do with it? Martha is young in spirit and always will be. [There is a knock at the door and MARTHA's voice calling: "May I come in, people?"] Sure thing! [BIGELOW jumps to open the door and MARTHA enters. She is flushed, excited, full of the joy of life, panting from her exertions.]

MARTHA—[Laughing.] I've had to run away and leave them with the governess. They're too active for me. [She throws herself on the couch.] Phew! I'm all tired out. I must be getting old.

CURTIS—[With a grin.] Big was just this minute remarking that, Martha. [BIGELOW looks embarrassed.]

MARTHA—[Laughing at him.] Well, I declare! Of all the horrid things to hear—

BIGELOW—[Still embarrassed but forcing a joking tone.] He—prevaricates, Mrs. Jayson.

MARTHA—There now, Curt! I'm sure it was you who said it. It sounds just like one of your horrid facts.

BIGELOW—And how can I offer my felicitations now? But I do,

116

despite your husband's calumny. May your shadow never grow less!

MARTHA—Thank you. [She shakes his proffered hand heartily.]

BIGELOW—And now I'll collect my flock and go home.

CURTIS—So long, Big. Be sure you don't mislay one of your heirs!

BIGELOW—No fear—but they might mislay me. [He goes. CURT sits down on couch. MARTHA goes to the window right, and looks out—after a pause, waving her hand.]

MARTHA—There they go. What darlings they are! [CURTIS grunts perfunctorily. MARTHA comes back and sits beside CURT on the couch—with a sigh.] Whoever did say it was right, Curt, I am getting old.

CURTIS—[Taking one of her hands and patting it.] Nonsense!

MARTHA—[Shaking her head and smiling with a touch of sadness.] No. I feel it.

CURTIS—[Puts his arms around her protectingly.] Nonsense! You're not the sort that ever grows old.

MARTHA—[Nestling up to him.] I'm afraid we're all that sort, dear. Even you. [She touches the white hair about his temples playfully.] Circumstantial evidence. I'll have to dye it when you're asleep some time—and then nobody'll know.

CURTIS—[Looking at her.] You haven't any silver threads. [Jokingly.] Am I to suspect—?

MARTHA—No, I don't. Honest, cross my heart, I wouldn't even conceal that from you, if I did. But gray hairs prove nothing. I am actually older than you, don't forget.

CURTIS—One whole year! That's frightful, isn't it?

MARTHA—I'm a woman, remember; so that one means at least six.

117

Ugh! Let's not talk about it. Do you know, it really fills me with a queer panic sometimes?

CURTIS—[Squeezing her.] Silly girl!

MARTHA—[Snuggling close to him.] Will you always love me—even when I'm old and ugly and feeble and you're still young and strong and handsome?

CURTIS—[Kisses her—tenderly.] Martha! What a foolish question, sweetheart. If we ever have to grow old, we'll do it together just as we've always done everything.

MARTHA—[With a happy sigh.] That's my dream of happiness, Curt. [Enthusiastically.] Oh, it has been a wonderful, strange life we've lived together, Curt, hasn't it? You're sure you've never regretted—never had the weest doubt that it might have been better with—someone else?

CURTIS—[Kisses her again—tenderly reproachful.] Martha!

MARTHA—And I have helped—really helped you, haven't I?

CURTIS—[Much moved.] You've been the best wife a man could ever wish for, Martha. You've been—you are wonderful. I owe everything to you—your sympathy and encouragement. Don't you know I realize that? [She kisses him gratefully.]

MARTHA—[Musing happily.] Yes, it's been a wonderful, glorious life. I'd live it over again if I could, every single second of it—even the terrible suffering—the children.

CURTIS—[Wincing.] Don't. I wouldn't want that over again. [Then changing the subject abruptly.] But why have you been putting all our life into the past tense? It seems to me the most interesting part is still ahead of us.

MARTHA—[Softly.] I mean—together—Curt.

CURTIS—So do I!

118

MARTHA—But you're going away—and I can't go with you this time.

CURTIS—[Smiling to himself over her head.] Yes, that does complicate matters, doesn't it?

MARTHA—[Hurt—looking up at him.] Curt! How indifferently you say that—as if you didn't care!

CURTIS—[Avoiding her eyes—teasingly.] What do you think you'll do all the time I'm gone?

MARTHA—Oh, I'll be lost—dead—I won't know what to do. I'll die of loneliness—[yearning creeping into her voice] unless—

CURTIS—[Inquisitively.] Unless what?

MARTHA—[Burying her face on his shoulder—passionately.] Oh, Curt, I love you so! Swear that you'll always love me no matter what I do—no matter what I ask—

CURTIS—[Vaguely uneasy now, trying to peer into her face.] But, sweetheart—

MARTHA—[Giving way weakly to her feelings for a moment—entreatingly.] Then don't go!

CURTIS—[Astonished.] Why, I've got to go. You know that.

MARTHA—Yes, I suppose you have. [Vigorously, as if flinging off a weakness.] Of course you have!

CURTIS—But, Martha—you said you'd be lonely unless—unless what?

MARTHA—Unless I— [She hesitates, blushing and confused.] I mean we—oh, I'm so afraid of what you'll—hold me close, very close to you and I'll whisper it. [She pulls his head down and whispers in his ear. A look of disappointment and aversion forces itself on his face.]

119

CURTIS—[Almost indignantly.] But that's impossible, Martha!

MARTHA—[Pleadingly.] Now don't be angry with me, Curt—not till you've heard everything. [With a trace of defiance.] It isn't impossible, Curt. It's so! It's happened! I was saving it as a secret—to tell you to-day—on my birthday.

CURTIS—[Stunned.] You mean it—is a fact?

MARTHA—Yes. [Then pitifully.] Oh, Curt, don't look that way! You seem so cold—so far away from me. [Straining her arms about him.] Why don't you hold me close to you? Why don't you say you're glad—for my sake?

CURTIS—[Agitatedly.] But Martha—you don't understand. How can I pretend gladness when—[Vehemently.] Why, it would spoil all our plans!

MARTHA—Plans? OUR plans? What do you mean?

CURTIS—[Excitedly.] Why, you're going with me, of course! I've obtained official permission. I've been working for it for months. The letter came yesterday morning.

MARTHA—[Stunned.] Permission—to go with you—

CURTIS—[Excitedly.] Yes. I couldn't conceive going without you. And I knew how you must be wishing—

MARTHA—[In pain.] Oh!

CURTIS—[Distractedly—jumping to his feet and staring at her bewilderedly.] Martha! You don't mean to tell me you weren't!

MARTHA—[In a crushed voice.] I was wishing you would finally decide not to go—to stay at home.

CURTIS—[Betraying exasperation.] But you must realize that's impossible. Martha, are you sure you've clearly understood what I've told you? You can go with me, do you hear? Everything is arranged. And I've had to fight so hard—I was running the risk of

120

losing my own chance by my insistence that I couldn't go without you.

MARTHA—[Weakly and helplessly.] I understand all that, Curt.

CURTIS—[Indignantly.] And yet—you hesitate! Why, this is the greatest thing of its kind ever attempted! There are unprecedented possibilities! A whole new world of knowledge may be opened up—the very origin of Man himself! And you will be the only woman—

MARTHA—I realize all that, Curt.

CURTIS—You can't—and hesitate! And then—think, Martha!—it will mean that you and I won't have to be separated. We can go on living the old, free life together.

MARTHA—[Growing calm now.] You are forgetting—what I told you, Curt. You must face the fact. I cannot go.

CURTIS—[Overwhelmed by the finality of her tone—after a pause.] How long have you known—this?

MARTHA—Two months, about.

CURTIS—But why didn't you tell me before?

MARTHA—I was afraid you wouldn't understand—and you haven't, Curt. But why didn't you tell me before—what you were planning?

CURTIS—[Eagerly.] You mean—then—you would have been glad to go—before this had happened?

MARTHA—I would have accepted it.

CURTIS—[Despairingly.] Martha, how could you ever have allowed this to happen? Oh, I suppose I'm talking foolishness. It wasn't your seeking, I know.

MARTHA—Yes it was, Curt. I wished it. I sought it.

121

CURTIS—[Indignantly.] Martha! [Then in a hurt tone.] You have broken the promise we made when they died. We were to keep their memories inviolate. They were to be always—our only children.

MARTHA—[Gently.] They forgive me, Curt. And you will forgive me, too—when you see him—and love him.

CURTIS—Him?

MARTHA—I know it will be a boy.

CURTIS—[Sinking down on the couch beside her—dully.] Martha! You have blown my world to bits.

MARTHA—[Taking one of his hands in hers—gently.] You must make allowances for me. Curt, and forgive me. I AM getting old. No, it's the truth. I've reached the turning point. Will you listen to my side of it, Curt, and try to see it—with sympathy—with true understanding—[With a trace of bitterness.]—forgetting your work for the moment?

CURTIS—[Miserably.] That's unfair, Martha. I think of it as OUR work—and I have always believed you did, too.

MARTHA—[Quickly.] I did, Curt! I do! All in the past is our work. It's my greatest pride to think so. But, Curt, I'll have to confess frankly—during the past two years I've felt myself—feeling as if I wasn't complete—with that alone.

CURTIS—Martha! [Bitterly.] And all the time I believed that more and more it was becoming the aim of your life, too.

MARTHA—[With a sad smile.] I'm glad of that, dear. I tried my best to conceal it from you. It would have been so unfair to let you guess while we were still in harness. But oh, how I kept looking forward to the time when we would come back—and rest—in our own home! You know—you said that was your plan—to stay here and write your books—and I was hoping—

122

CURTIS—[With a gesture of aversion.] I loathe this book-writing. It isn't my part, I realize now. But when I made the plans you speak of, how could I know that then?

MARTHA—[Decisively.] You've got to go. I won't try to stop you. I'll help all in my power—as I've always done. Only—I can't go with you any more. And you must help me—to do my work—by understanding it. [He is silent, frowning, his face agitated, preoccupied. She goes on intensely.] Oh, Curt, I wish I could tell you what I feel, make you feel with me the longing for a child. If you had just the tiniest bit of feminine in you—! [Forcing a smile.] But you're so utterly masculine, dear! That's what has made me love you, I suppose—so I've no right to complain of it. [Intensely.] I don't. I wouldn't have you changed one bit! I love you! And I love the things you love—your work—because it's a part of you. And that's what I want you to do—to reciprocate—to love the creator in me—to desire that I, too, should complete myself with the thing nearest my heart!

CURTIS—[Intensely preoccupied with his own struggle—vaguely.] But I thought—

MARTHA—I know; but, after all, your work is yours, not mine. I have been only a helper, a good comrade, too, I hope, but—somehow—outside of it all. Do you remember two years ago when we were camped in Yunnan, among the aboriginal tribes? It was one night there when we were lying out in our sleeping-bags up in the mountains along the Tibetan frontier. I couldn't sleep. Suddenly I felt oh, so tired—utterly alone—out of harmony with you—with the earth under me. I became horribly despondent—like an outcast who suddenly realizes the whole world is alien. And all the wandering about the world, and all the romance and excitement I'd enjoyed in it, appeared an aimless, futile business, chasing around in a circle in an effort to avoid touching reality. Forgive me, Curt. I meant myself, not you, of course. Oh, it was horrible, I tell you, to feel that way. I tried to laugh at myself, to fight it off, but it stayed and grew worse. It seemed as if I were the only creature alive—who was not alive. And all at once the picture came of a tribeswoman who stood looking at us in a little mountain village as we rode by. She was nursing her child. Her eyes were so curiously sure of herself. She was horribly ugly, poor woman, and yet—as the picture came back to me—I appeared to myself the ugly one while she was beautiful. And I thought of our children who had died—and such a longing for another child came to me that I began sobbing. You were asleep. You didn't hear. [She pauses—then proceeds slowly.] And when we came back here—to have a home at last, I was so happy because I saw my chance of fulfillment—before it was too late. [In a gentle, pleading voice.] Now can you understand, dear? [She puts her hand on his arm.]

CURTIS—[Starting as if awaking from a sleep.] Understand? No, I can't understand, Martha.

MARTHA—[In a gasp of unbearable hurt.] Curt! I don't believe you heard a word I was saying.

CURTIS—[Bursting forth as if releasing all the pent-up struggle that has been gathering within him.] No, I can't understand. I cannot, cannot! It seems like treachery to me.

MARTHA—Curt!

CURTIS—I've depended on you. This is the crucial point—the biggest thing of my life—and you desert me!

MARTHA—[Resentment gathering in her eyes.] If you had listened to me—if you had even tried to feel—

CURTIS—I feel that you are deliberately ruining my highest hope. How can I go on without you? I've been trying to imagine myself alone. I can't! Even with my work—who can I get to take your place? Oh, Martha, why do you have to bring this new element into our lives at this late day? Haven't we been sufficient, you and I together? Isn't that a more difficult, beautiful happiness to achieve than—children? Everyone has children. Don't I love you as much as any man could love a woman? Isn't that enough for you? Doesn't it mean anything to you that I need you so terribly—for myself, for

124

my work—for everything that is best and worthiest in me? Can you expect me to be glad when you propose to introduce a stranger who will steal away your love, your interest—who will separate us and deprive me of you! No, no, I cannot! It's asking the impossible. I am only human.

MARTHA—If you were human you would think of my life as well as yours.

CURTIS—I do! It is OUR life I am fighting for, not mine—OUR life that you want to destroy.

MARTHA—Our life seems to mean your life to you, Curt—and only your life. I have devoted fifteen years to that. Now I must fight for my own.

CURTIS—[Aghast.] You talk as if we were enemies, Martha! [Striding forward and seizing her in his arms.] No, you don't mean it! I love you so, Martha! You've made yourself part of my life, my work—I need you so! I can't share you with anyone! I won't! Martha, my own! Say that you won't, dear? [He kisses her passionately again and again.]

MARTHA—[All her love and tenderness aroused by his kisses and passionate sincerity—weakening.] Curt! Curt! [Pitiably.] It won't separate us, dear. Can't you see he will be a link between us—even when we are away from each other—that he will bring us together all the closer?

CURTIS—But I can't be away from you!

MARTHA—[Miserably.] Oh, Curt, why won't you look the fact in the face—and learn to accept it with joy? Why can't you for my sake? I would do that for you.

CURTIS—[Breaking away from her—passionately.] You will not do what I have implored you—for me! And I am looking the fact in the face—the fact that there must be no fact! [Avoiding her eyes—as if defying his own finer feelings.] There are doctors who—

125

MARTHA—[Shrinking back from him.] Curt! You propose that—to me! [With overwhelming sorrow.] Oh, Curt! When I feel him—his life within me—like a budding of my deepest soul—to flower and continue me—you say what you have just said! [Grief-stricken.] Oh, you never, never, never will understand!

CURTIS—[Shamefacedly.] Martha, I—[Distractedly.] I don't know what I'm saying! This whole situation is so unbearable! Why, why does it have to happen now?

MARTHA—[Gently.] It must be now—or not at all—at my age, dear. [Then after a pause—staring at him frightenedly—sadly.] You have changed, Curt. I remember it used to be your happiness to sacrifice yourself for me.

CURTIS—I had no work then—no purpose beyond myself. To sacrifice oneself is easy. But when your only meaning becomes as a searcher for knowledge—you cannot sacrifice that, Martha. You must sacrifice everything for that—or lose all sincerity.

MARTHA—I wonder where your work leaves off and you begin. Hasn't your work become you?

CURTIS—Yes and no. [Helplessly.] You can't understand, Martha!...

MARTHA—Nor you.

CURTIS—[With a trace of bitter irony.] And you and your work? Aren't they one and the same?

MARTHA—So you think mine is selfish, too? [After a pause— sadly.] I can't blame you, Curt. It's all my fault. I've spoiled you by giving up my life so completely to yours. You've forgotten I have one. Oh, I don't mean that I was a martyr. I know that in you alone lay my happiness and fulfillment in those years—after the children died. But we are no longer what we were then. We must, both of us, relearn to love and respect—what we have become.

CURTIS—[Violently.] Nonsense! You talk as if love were an

126

intellectual process—[Taking her into his arms—passionately.] I love you—always and forever! You are me and I am you. What use is all this vivisecting? [He kisses her fiercely. They look into each other's eyes for a second—then instinctively fall back from one another.]

MARTHA—[In a whisper.] Yes, you love me. But who am I? There is no recognition in your eyes. You don't know.

CURTIS—[Frightenedly.] Martha! Stop! This is terrible! [They continue to be held by each other's fearfully questioning eyes.]

[The Curtain Falls]

ACT III

SCENE—Same as Act II. As the curtain rises, JAYSON is discovered sitting in an armchair by the fireplace, in which a log fire is burning fitfully. He is staring into the flames, a strained, expectant expression on his face. It is about three o'clock in the morning. There is no light but that furnished by the fire which fills the room with shifting shadows. The door in the rear is opened and RICHARD appears, his face harried by the stress of unusual emotion. Through the opened doorway, a low, muffled moan of anguish sounds from the upper part of the house. JAYSON and RICHARD both shudder. The latter closes the door behind him quickly as if anxious to shut out the noise.

JAYSON—[Looking up anxiously.] Well?

RICHARD—[Involuntarily straightening up as if about to salute and report to a superior officer.] No change, sir. [Then, as if remembering himself, comes to the fireplace and slumps down in a chair—agitatedly.] God, Dad, I can't stand her moaning and screaming! It's got my nerves shot to pieces. I thought I was hardened. I've heard them out in No Man's Land—dying by inches—when you couldn't get to them or help—but this is worse—a million times! After all, that was war—and they were men—

JAYSON—Martha is having an exceptionally hard ordeal.

RICHARD—Since three o'clock this morning—yesterday morning, I should say. It's a wonder she isn't dead.

JAYSON—[After a pause.] Where is Curt?

RICHARD—[Harshly.] Still out in the garden, walking around bareheaded in the cold like a lunatic.

128

JAYSON—Why didn't you make him come in?

RICHARD—Make him! It's easy to say. He's in a queer state, Dad, I can tell you! There's something torturing him besides her pain—

JAYSON—[After a pause.] Yes, there's a lot in all this we don't know about.

RICHARD—I suppose the reason he's so down on the family is because we've rather cut her since that tea affair.

JAYSON—He shouldn't blame us. She acted abominably and has certainly caused enough talk since then—always about with Bigelow—

RICHARD—[With a sardonic laugh.] And yet he keeps asking everyone to send for Bigelow—says he wants to talk to him—not us. WE can't understand! [He laughs bitterly.]

JAYSON—I'm afraid Curt knows we understand too much. [Agitatedly.] But why does he want Bigelow, in God's name? In his present state—with the suspicions he must have—there's liable to be a frightful scene.

RICHARD—Don't be afraid of a scene. [With pitying scorn.] The hell of it is he seems to regard Bigelow as his best friend. Damned if I can make it out.

JAYSON—I gave orders that they were always to tell Curt Bigelow was out of town and couldn't be reached. [With a sigh.] What a frightful situation for all of us! [After a pause.] It may sound cruel of me—but—I can't help wishing for all our sakes that this child will never—

RICHARD—Yes, Dad, I know what you're thinking. It would be the best thing for it, too—although I hate myself for saying it. [There is a pause. Then the door in rear is opened and LILY appears. She is pale and agitated. Leaving the door open behind her she comes forward and flings herself on the lounge.]

129

JAYSON—[Anxiously.] Well?

LILY—[Irritably, getting up and switching on the lights.] Isn't everything gloomy enough? [Sits down.] I couldn't bear it upstairs one second longer. Esther and Emily are coming down, too. It's too much for them—and they've had personal experience. [Trying to mask her agitation by a pretense at flippancy.] I hereby become a life-member of the birth-control league. Let's let humanity cease—if God can't manage its continuance any better than that!

RICHARD—[Seriously.] Second the motion.

JAYSON—[Peevishly.] You're young idiots. Keep your blasphemous nonsense to yourself, Lily!

LILY—[Jumping up and stamping her foot—hysterically.] I can't stand it. Take me home, Dick, won't you? We're doing no good waiting here. I'll have a fit—or something—if I stay.

RICHARD—[Glad of the excuse to go himself—briskly.] That's how I feel. I'll drive you home. Come along. [ESTHER and EMILY enter, followed by JOHN.]

LILY—[Excitedly.] I'll never marry or have a child! Never, never! I'll go into Mark's office to-morrow and make myself independent of marriage.

ESTHER—Sssh! Lily! Don't you know you're shouting? And what silly talk!

LILY—I'll show you whether it's silly! I'll—

RICHARD—[Impatiently.] Are you coming or not?

LILY—[Quickly.] Yes—wait—here I am. [She pushes past the others and follows RICHARD out rear. ESTHER and EMILY sit on couch—JOHN on chair, right rear.]

ESTHER—[With a sigh.] I thought I went through something when mine were born—but this is too awful.

130

EMILY—And, according to John, Curt actually says he hates it! Isn't that terrible? [After a pause—meaningly.] It's almost as if her suffering was a punishment, don't you think?

ESTHER—If it is, she's being punished enough, Heaven knows. It can't go on this way much longer or something dreadful will happen.

EMILY—Do you think the baby—

ESTHER—I don't know. I shouldn't say it but perhaps it would be better if—

EMILY—That's what I think.

ESTHER—Oh, I wish I didn't have such evil suspicions—but the way Curt goes on—how can you help feeling there's something wrong?

JAYSON—[Suddenly.] How is Curt?

EMILY—John just came in from the garden. [Turning around to where JOHN is dozing in his chair—sharply.] John! Well I never! If he isn't falling asleep! John! [He jerks up his head and stares at her, blinking stupidly. She continues irritably.] A nice time to pick out for a nap, I must say.

JOHN—[Surlily.] Don't forget I have to be at the bank in the morning.

JAYSON—[Testily.] I have to be at the bank, too—and you don't notice me sleeping. Tell me about Curt. You just left him, didn't you?

JOHN—[Irritably.] Yes, and I've been walking around that damned garden half the night watching over him. Isn't that enough to wear anyone out? I can feel I've got a terrible cold coming on—

ESTHER—[Impatiently.] For goodness sake, don't you start to pity yourself!

131

JOHN—[Indignantly.] I'm not. I think I've showed my willingness to do everything I could. If Curt was only the least bit grateful! He isn't. He hates us all and wishes we were out of his home. I would have left long ago if I didn't want to do my part in saving the family name from disgrace.

JAYSON—[Impatiently.] Has he quieted down, that's what I want to know?

JOHN—[Harshly.] Not the least bit. He's out of his head—and I'd be out of mine if a child was being born to my wife that—

JAYSON—[Angrily.] Keep that to yourself! Remember you have no proof. [Morosely.] Think all you want—but don't talk.

EMILY—[Pettishly.] The whole town knows it, anyway; I'm sure they must.

JAYSON—There's only been gossip—no real scandal. Let's do our united best to keep it at that. [After a pause.] Where's Aunt Elizabeth? We'll have to keep an eye on her, too, or she's quite liable to blurt out the whole business before all comers.

ESTHER—You needn't be afraid. She's forgotten all about the scandalous part. No word of it has come to her out in the country and she hasn't set foot in town since that unfortunate tea, remember. And at present she's so busy wishing the child will be a boy, that she hasn't a thought for another thing. [The door in the rear is opened and MARK SHEFFIELD enters. He comes up to the fire to warm himself. The others watch him in silence for a moment.]

JAYSON—[Impatiently.] Well, Mark? Where's Curt?

SHEFFIELD—[Frowning.] Inside. I think he'll be with us in a minute. [With a scornful smile.] Just now he's 'phoning to Bigelow. [The others gasp.]

JAYSON—[Furiously.] For God's sake, couldn't you stop him?

132

SHEFFIELD—Not without a scene. Your Aunt persuaded him to come into the house—and he rushed for the 'phone. I think he guessed we had been lying to him—

JAYSON—[After a pause.] Then he—Bigelow will be here soon?

SHEFFIELD—[Drily.] It depends on his sense of decency. As he seems lacking in that quality, I've no doubt he'll come.

JOHN—[Rising to his feet—pompously.] Then I, for one, will go. Come, Emily. Since Curt seems bound to disgrace everyone concerned, I want it thoroughly understood that we wash our hands of the whole disgraceful affair.

EMILY—[Snappishly.] Go if you want to! I won't! [Then with a sacrificing air.] I think it is our duty to stay.

JAYSON—[Exasperated.] Sit down. Wash your hands indeed! Aren't you as much concerned as any of us?

SHEFFIELD—[Sharply.] Sshh! I think I hear Curt now. [JOHN sits down abruptly. All stiffen into stony attitudes. The door is opened and CURT enters. He is incredibly drawn and haggard, a tortured, bewildered expression in his eyes. His hair is dishevelled, his boots caked with mud. He stands at the door staring from one to the other of his family with a wild, contemptuous scorn and mutters.]

CURTIS—Liars! Well, he's coming now. [Then bewilderedly.] Why didn't you want him to come, eh? He's my oldest friend. I've got to talk to someone—and I can't to you. [Wildly.] What do you want here, anyway? Why don't you go? [A scream of MARTHA's is heard through the doorway. CURT shudders violently, slams the door to with a crash, putting his shoulders against it as if to bar out the sound inexorably—in anguish.] God, why must she go through such agony? Why? Why? [He goes to the fireplace as MARK makes way for him, flings himself exhaustedly on a chair, his shoulders bowed, his face hidden in his hands. The others stare at him pityingly. There is a long silence. Then the two women whisper together, get up and tiptoe out of the room, motioning for the

133

others to follow them. JOHN does so. SHEFFIELD starts to go, then notices the preoccupied JAYSON who is staring moodily into the fire.]

SHEFFIELD—Sstt! [As JAYSON looks up—in a whisper.] Let's go out and leave him alone. Perhaps he'll sleep.

JAYSON—[Starting to follow SHEFFIELD, hesitates and puts a hand on his son's shoulder.] Curt. Remember I'm your father. Can't you confide in me? I'll do anything to help.

CURTIS—[Harshly.] No, Dad. Leave me alone.

JAYSON—[Piqued.] As you wish. [He starts to go.]

CURTIS—And send Big in to me as soon as he comes.

JAYSON—[Stops, appears about to object—then remarks coldly.] Very well—if you insist. [He switches off the lights. He hesitates at the door uncertainly, then opens it and goes out. There is a pause. Then CURT lifts his head and peers about the room. Seeing he is alone he springs to his feet and begins to pace back and forth, his teeth clenched, his features working convulsively. Then, as if attracted by an irresistible impulse, he goes to the closed door and puts his ear to the crack. He evidently hears his wife's moans for he starts away—in agony.]

CURTIS—Oh, Martha, Martha! Martha, darling! [He flings himself in the chair by the fireplace—hides his face in his hands and sobs bitterly. There is a ring from somewhere in the house. Soon after there is a knock at the door. CURTIS doesn't hear at first but when it is repeated he mutters huskily.] Come in. [BIGELOW enters. CURT looks up at him.] Close that door, Big, for God's sake!

BIGELOW—[Does so—then taking off his overcoat, hat, and throwing them on the lounge comes quickly over to CURT.] I got over as soon as I could. [As he sees CURT's face he starts and says sympathetically.] By Jove, old man, you look as though you'd been through hell!

134

CURTIS—[Grimly.] I have. I am.

BIGELOW—[Slapping his back.] Buck up! [Then anxiously.] How's Martha?

CURTIS—She's in hell, too—

BIGELOW—[Attempting consolation.] You're surely not worrying, are you? Martha is so strong and healthy there's no doubt of her pulling through in fine shape.

CURTIS—She should never have attempted this. [After a pause.] I've a grudge against you, Big. It was you bringing your children over here that first planted this in her mind.

BIGELOW—[After a pause.] I've guessed you thought that. That's why you haven't noticed me—or them—over here so much lately. I'll confess that I felt you—[Angrily.] And the infernal gossip—I'll admit I thought that you—oh, damn this rotten town, anyway!

CURTIS—[Impatiently.] Oh, for God's sake! [Bitterly.] I didn't want you here to discuss Bridgetown gossip.

BIGELOW—I know, old man, forgive me. [In spite of the closed door one of MARTHA's agonized moans is heard. They both shudder.]

CURTIS—[In a dead, monotonous tone.] She has been moaning like that hour after hour. I shall have those sounds in my ears until the day I die. Nothing can ever make me forget—nothing.

BIGELOW—[Trying to distract him.] Deuce take it, Curt, what's the matter with you? I never thought you'd turn morbid.

CURTIS—[Darkly.] I've changed, Big—I hardly know myself any more.

BIGELOW—Once you're back on the job again, you'll be all right. You're still determined to go on this expedition, aren't you?

CURTIS—Yes. I was supposed to join them this week in New York

135

but I've arranged to catch up with them in China—as soon as it's possible for us to go.

BIGELOW—Us? You mean you still plan to take—

CURTIS—[Angrily aggressive.] Yes, certainly! Why not? Martha ought to be able to travel in a month or so.

BIGELOW—Yes, but—do you think it would be safe to take the child?

CURTIS—[With a bitter laugh.] Yes—I was forgetting the child, wasn't I? [Viciously.] But perhaps—[Then catching himself with a groan.] Oh, damn all children, Big!

BIGELOW—[Astonished.] Curt!

CURTIS—[In anguish.] I can't help it—I've fought against it. But it's there—deep down in me—and I can't drive it out. I can't!

BIGELOW—[Bewildered.] What, Curt?

CURTIS—Hatred! Yes, hatred! What's the use of denying it? I must tell someone and you're the only one who might understand. [With a wild laugh.] For you—hated your wife, didn't you?

BIGELOW—[Stunned.] Good God, you don't mean you hate—Martha?

CURTIS—[Raging.] Hate Martha? How dare you, you fool! I love Martha—love her with every miserable drop of blood in me—with all my life—all my soul! She is my whole world—everything! Hate Martha! God, man, have you gone crazy to say such a mad thing? [Savagely.] No. I hate it. It!

BIGELOW—[Shocked.] Curt! Don't you know you can't talk like that—now—when—CURTIS— [Harshly.] It has made us both suffer torments—not only now—every day, every hour, for months and months. Why shouldn't I hate it, eh?

136

BIGELOW—[Staring at his friend's wild, distorted face with growing horror.] Curt! Can't you realize how horrible—

CURTIS—Yes, it's horrible. I've told myself that a million times. [With emphasis.] But it's true!

BIGELOW—[Severely.] Shut up! You're not yourself. Come, think for a moment. What would Martha feel if she heard you going on this way? Why—it would kill her!

CURTIS—[With a sobbing groan.] Oh, I know, I know! [After a pause.] She read it in my eyes. Yes, it's horrible, but when I saw her there suffering so frightfully—I couldn't keep it out of my eyes. I tried to force it back—for her sake—but I couldn't. I was holding her hands and her eyes searched mine with such a longing question in them—and she read only my hatred there, not my love for her. And she screamed and seemed to try to push me away. I wanted to kneel down and pray for forgiveness—to tell her it was only my love for her—that I couldn't help it. And then the doctors told me to leave—and now the door is locked against me—[He sobs.]

BIGELOW—[Greatly moved.] This is only your damned imagination. They put you out because you were in their way, that's all. And as for Martha, she was probably suffering so much—

CURTIS—No. She read it in my eyes. I saw that look in hers—of horror—horror of me!

BIGELOW—[Gruffly.] You're raving, damn it!

CURTIS—[Unheeding.] It came home to her then—the undeniable truth. [With a groan.] Isn't it fiendish that I should be the one to add to her torture—in spite of myself—in spite of all my will to conceal it! She will never forgive me, never! And how can I forgive myself?

BIGELOW—[Distractedly.] For God's sake, don't think about it! It's absurd—ridiculous!

CURTIS—[Growing more calm—in a tone of obsession.] She's guessed it ever since that day when we quarreled—her birthday.

137

Oh, you can have no idea of the misery there has been in our lives since then. You haven't seen or guessed the reason. No one has. It has been—the thought of IT.

BIGELOW—Curt!

CURTIS—[Unheeding.] For years we had welded our lives together so that we two were sufficient, each to each. There was no room for a third. And it was a fine, free life we had made—a life of new worlds, of discovery, of knowledge invaluable to mankind. Isn't such a life worth all the sacrifice it must entail?

BIGELOW—But that life was your life, Curt—

CURTIS—[Vehemently.] No, it was her life, too—her work as well as mine. She had made the life, our life—the work, our work. Had she the right to repudiate what she had built because she suddenly has a fancy for a home, children, a miserable ease! I had thought I was her home, her children. I had tried to make my life worthy of being that to her. And I had failed. I was not enough.

BIGELOW—Curt!

CURTIS—Oh, I tried to become reconciled. I tried my damnedest. I tried to love this child as I had loved those that died. But I couldn't. And so, this being estranged us. We loved as intensely as ever but IT pushed us apart. I grew to dread the idea of this intruder. She saw this in me. I denied it—but she knew. There was something in each of us the other grew to hate. And still we loved as never before, perhaps, for we grew to pity each other's helplessness.

BIGELOW—Curt! Are you sure you ought to tell anyone this?

CURTIS—[Waving his remark aside.] One day, when I was trying to imagine myself without her, and finding nothing but hopelessness—yet knowing I must go—a thought suddenly struck me—a horrible but fascinating possibility that had never occurred to me before. [With feverish intensity.] Can you guess what it was?

138

BIGELOW—No. And I think you've done enough morbid raving, if you ask me.

CURTIS—The thought that came to me was that if a certain thing happened, Martha could still go with me. And I knew, if it did happen, that she would want to go, that she would fling herself into the spirit of our work to forget, that she would be mine more than ever.

BIGELOW—[Afraid to believe the obvious answer.] Curt!

CURTIS—Yes. My thought was that the child might be born dead.

BIGELOW—[Repelled—sternly.] Damn it, man, do you know what you're saying? [Relentingly.] No, Curt, old boy, do stop talking. If you don't I'll send for a doctor, damned if I won't. That talk belongs in an asylum. God, man, can't you realize this is your child—yours as well as hers?

CURTIS—I've tried. I cannot. There is some inexorable force in me—

BIGELOW—[Coldly.] Do you realize how contemptible this confession makes you out? [Angrily.] Why, if you had one trace of human kindness in you—one bit of unselfish love for your wife—one particle of pity for her suffering—

CURTIS—[Anguished.] I have—all the love and pity in the world for her! That's why I can't help hating—the cause of her suffering.

BIGELOW—Have you never thought that you might repay Martha for giving up all her life to you by devoting the rest of yours to her?

CURTIS—[Bitterly.] She can be happy without me. She will have this child—to take my place. [Intensely.] You think I would not give up my work for her? But I would! I will stay here—do anything she wishes—if only we can make a new beginning again—together—ALONE!

BIGELOW—[Agitated.] Curt, for God's sake, don't return to that!

Why, good God, man—even now—while you're speaking—don't you realize what may be happening? And you can talk as if you were wishing—

CURTIS—[Fiercely.] I can't help but wish it!

BIGELOW—[Distractedly.] For the love of God, if you have such thoughts, keep them to yourself. I won't listen! You make me despise life!

CURTIS—And would you have me love life? [The door in the rear is opened and JAYSON enters, pale and unnerved. A succession of quick, piercing shrieks is heard before he can close the door behind him. Shuddering.] My God! My God! [With a fierce cry.] Will—this—never—end!

JAYSON—[Tremblingly.] Sh-h-h, they say this is the crisis. [Puts his arm around CURT.] Bear up, my boy, it will soon be over now. [He sits down in the chair BIGELOW has vacated, pointedly ignoring the latter. The door is opened again and EMILY, ESTHER, JOHN and SHEFFIELD file in quickly as if escaping from the cries of the woman upstairs. They are all greatly agitated. CURT groans, pressing his clenched fists against his ears. The two women sit on the lounge. MARK comes forward and stands by JAYSON'S chair, JOHN sits by the door as before. BIGELOW retreats behind CURT's chair, aware of their hostility. There is a long pause.]

ESTHER—[Suddenly.] She has stopped—[They all listen.]

JAYSON—[Huskily.] Thank God, it's over at last. [The door is opened and MRS. DAVIDSON enters. The old lady is radiant, weeping tears of joy.]

MRS. DAVIDSON—[Calls out exultantly between sobs.] A son, Curt—a son. [With rapt fervor—falling on her knees.] Let us all give thanks to God!

CURTIS—[In a horrible cry of rage and anguish.] No! No! You lie! [They all cry out in fright and amazement: "CURT!" The door is opened and the NURSE appears.]

140

NURSE—[Looking at CURTIS, in a low voice.] Mr. Jayson, your wife is asking for you.

BIGELOW—[Promptly slapping CURT on the back.] There! What did I tell you? Run, you chump!

CURTIS—[With a gasp of joy.] Martha! Darling, I'm coming—[He rushes out after the NURSE.]

BIGELOW—[Comes forward to get his hat and coat from the sofa— coldly.] Pardon me, please. [They shrink away from him.]

EMILY—[As he goes to the door—cuttingly.] Some people seem to have no sense of decency!

BIGELOW—[Stung, stops at the door and looks from one to the other of them—bitingly.] No, I quite agree with you. [He goes out, shutting the door. They all gasp angrily.]

JOHN—Scoundrel!

JAYSON—[Testily—going to MRS. D., who is still on her knees praying.] Do get up, Aunt Elizabeth! How ridiculous! What a scene if anyone should see you like that. [He raises her to her feet and leads her to a chair by the fire. She obeys unresistingly, seemingly unaware of what she is doing.]

ESTHER—[Unable to restrain her jealousy.] So it's a boy.

EMILY—Did you hear Curt—how he yelled out "No"? It's plain as the nose on your face he didn't want—

ESTHER—How awful!

JOHN—Well, can you blame him?

EMILY—And the awful cheek of that Bigelow person—coming here—

ESTHER—They appeared as friendly as ever when we came in.

141

JOHN—[Scornfully.] Curt is a blind simpleton—and that man is a dyed-in-the-wool scoundrel.

JAYSON—[Frightenedly.] Shhh! Suppose we were overheard!

EMILY—When Curt leaves we can put her in her proper place. I'll soon let her know she hasn't fooled me, for one. [While she is speaking MRS. D. has gotten up and is going silently toward the door.]

JAYSON—[Testily.] Aunt Elizabeth, where are you going?

MRS. D.—[Tenderly.] I must see him again, the dear! [She goes out.]

ESTHER—[Devoured by curiosity—hesitatingly.] I think I—come on, Emily. Let's go up and see—

EMILY—Not I! I never want to lay eyes on it.

JOHN—Nor I.

ESTHER—I was only thinking—everyone will think it funny if we don't.

JAYSON—[Hastily.] Yes, yes. We must keep up appearances. [Getting to his feet.] Yes, I think we had better all go up—make some sort of inquiry about Martha, you know. It's expected of us and—[They are all standing, hesitating, when the door in the rear is opened and the NURSE appears, supporting CURT. The latter is like a corpse. His face is petrified with grief, his body seems limp and half-paralyzed.]

NURSE—[Her eyes flashing, indignantly.] It's a wonder some of you wouldn't come up—here, help me! Take him, can't you? I've got to run back!

[JAYSON and SHEFFIELD spring forward and lead CURT to a chair by the fire.]

JAYSON—[Anxious.] Curt! Curt, my boy! What is it, son?

142

EMILY—[Catching the NURSE as she tries to go.] Nurse! What is the matter?

NURSE—[Slowly.] His wife is dead. [They are all still, stunned.] She lived just long enough to recognize him.

EMILY—And—the baby?

NURSE—[With a professional air.] Oh, it's a fine, healthy baby— eleven pounds—that's what made it so difficult. [She goes. The others all stand in silence.]

ESTHER—[Suddenly sinking on the couch and bursting into tears.] Oh, I'm so sorry I said—or thought—anything wrong about her. Forgive me, Martha!

SHEFFIELD—[Honestly moved but unable to resist this opportunity for Latin—solemnly.] De mortuis nil nisi bonum.

JAYSON—[Who has been giving all his attention to his son.] Curt! Curt! EMILY—Hadn't the doctor better—

JAYSON—Shhh! He begins to recognize me. Curt!

CURTIS—[Looking around him bewilderedly.] Yes. [Suddenly remembrance comes and a spasm of intolerable pain contracts his features. He presses his hands to the side of his head and groans brokenly.] Martha! Gone! Dead! Oh! [He appeals wildly to the others.] Her eyes—she knew me—she smiled—she whispered— forgive me, Curt,—forgive her—when it was I who should have said forgive me—but before I could—she—[He falters brokenly.]

EMILY—[Looking from one to the other meaningly as if this justified all their suspicions.] Oh!

CURTIS—[A sudden triumph in his voice.] But she loved me again—only me—I saw it in her eyes! She had forgotten—IT. [Raging.] Never let me see it! Never let it come near me! It has murdered her! [Springing to his feet.] I hate it from the bottom of my soul—I will never see it—never—never—I take my oath! [As his father takes his arm—shaking him off.] Let me go! I am going back to her! [He strides out of the door in a frenzy of grief and rage. They all stand transfixed, looking at each other bewilderedly.]

EMILY—[Putting all her venomous gratification into one word.] Well!

[The Curtain Falls]

ACT IV

SCENE—Same as Act I. It is afternoon of a fine day three days later. Motors are heard coming up the drive in front of the house. There is the muffled sound of voices. The MAID is seen going along the hall to the front door. Then the family enter from the rear. First come JAYSON and ESTHER with MRS. DAVIDSON—then LILY, DICK and SHEFFIELD—then JOHN and his wife. All are dressed in mourning. The only one who betrays any signs of sincere grief is MRS. DAVIDSON. The others all have a strained look, irritated, worried, or merely gloomy. They seem to be thinking "The worst is yet to come."

JAYSON—[Leading MRS. D., who is weeping softly, to the chair at left of table—fretfully.] Please do sit down, Aunt. [She does so mechanically.] And do stop crying. [He sits down in front of table. ESTHER goes to couch where she is joined by EMILY. MARK goes over and stands in back of them. DICK and JOHN sit at rear of table. LILY comes down front and walks about nervously. She seems in a particularly fretful, upset mood.]

LILY—[Trying to conceal her feelings under a forced flippancy.] What ridiculous things funerals are, anyway! That stupid minister—whining away through his nose! Why does the Lord show such a partiality for men with adenoids, I wonder.

JAYSON—[Testily.] Sshhh! Have you no respect for anything?

LILY—[Resentfully.] If I had, I'd have lost it when I saw all of you pulling such long faces in the church where you knew you were under observation. Pah! Such hypocrisy! And then, to cap it all, Emily has to force out a few crocodile tears at the grave!

EMILY—[Indignantly.] When I saw Curt—that's why I cried—not for her!

145

JAYSON—What a scene Curt made! I actually believe he wanted to throw himself into the grave!

DICK—You BELIEVE he wanted to! Why, it was all Mark and I could do to hold him, wasn't it, Mark? [SHEFFIELD nods.]

JAYSON—Intolerable! I never expected he'd turn violent like that. He's seemed calm enough the past three days.

LILY—Calm! Yes, just like a corpse is calm!

JAYSON—[Distractedly.] And now this perfectly mad idea of going away to-day to join that infernal expedition—leaving that child on our hands—the child he has never even looked at! Why, it's too monstrously flagrant! He's deliberately flaunting this scandal in everyone's face!

JOHN—[Firmly.] He must be brought to time.

SHEFFIELD—Yes, we must talk to him—quite openly, if we're forced to. After all, I guess he realizes the situation more keenly than any of us.

LILY—[Who has wandered to window on right.] You mean you think he believes—Well, I don't. And you had better be careful not to let him guess what you think. [Pointing outside.] There's my proof. There he is walking about with Bigelow. Can you imagine Curt doing that—if he thought for a moment—

DICK—Oh, I guess Curt isn't all fool. He knows that's the very best way to keep people from suspecting.

ESTHER—[Indignantly.] But wouldn't you think that Bigelow person—It's disgusting, his sticking to Curt like this.

SHEFFIELD—Well, for one, I'm becoming quite resigned to Bigelow's presence. In the first place, he seems to be the only one who can bring Curt to reason. Then again, I feel that it is to Bigelow's own interest to convince Curt that he mustn't provoke an open scandal by running away without acknowledging this child.

146

LILY—[Suddenly bursting forth hysterically.] Oh, I hate you, all of you! I loathe your suspicions—and I loathe myself because I'm beginning to be poisoned by them, too.

EMILY—Really, Lily, at this late hour—after the way Curt has acted—and her last words when she was dying—

LILY—[Distractedly.] I know! Shut up! Haven't you told it a million times already? [MRS. DAVIDSON gets up and walks to the door, rear. She has been crying softly during this scene, oblivious to the talk around her.]

JAYSON—[Testily.] Aunt Elizabeth! Where are you going? [As she doesn't answer but goes out into the hall.] Esther, go with her and see that she doesn't—

ESTHER—[Gets up with a jealous irritation.] She's only going up to see the baby. She's simply forgotten everything else in the world!

LILY—[Indignantly.] She probably realizes what we are too mean to remember—that the baby, at least, is innocent. Wait, Esther. I'll come with you.

JAYSON—Yes, hurry, she shouldn't be left alone. [ESTHER and LILY follow the old lady out, rear.]

DICK—[After a pause—impatiently.] Well, what next? I don't see what good we are accomplishing. May I run along? [He gets up restlessly as he is speaking and goes to the window.]

JAYSON—[Severely.] You will stay, if you please. There's to be no shirking on anyone's part. It may take all of us to induce Curt—

SHEFFIELD—I wouldn't worry. Bigelow is taking that job off our hands, I imagine.

DICK—[Looking out of the window.] He certainly seems to be doing his damnedest. [With a sneer.] The stage missed a great actor in him.

147

JAYSON—[Worriedly.] But, if Bigelow should fail—

SHEFFIELD—Then we'll succeed. [With a grim smile.] By God, we'll have to.

JAYSON—Curt has already packed his trunks and had them taken down to the station—told me he was leaving on the five o'clock train.

SHEFFIELD—But didn't you hint to him there was now this matter of the child to be considered in making his plans?

JAYSON—[Lamely.] I started to. He simply flared up at me with insane rage.

DICK—[Looking out the window.] Say, I believe they're coming in.

JAYSON—Bigelow?

DICK—Yes, they're both making for the front door.

SHEFFIELD—I suggest we beat a retreat to Curt's study and wait there.

JAYSON—Yes, let's do that—come on, all of you. [They all retire grumblingly but precipitately to the study, closing the door behind them. The front door is heard opening and a moment later CURT and BIGELOW enter the room. CURT's face is set in an expression of stony grief. BIGELOW is flushed, excited, indignant.]

BIGELOW—[As CURT sinks down on the couch—pleading indignantly.] Curt, damn it, wake up! Are you made of stone? Has everything I've said gone in one ear and out the other? I know it's hell for me to torment you at this particular time but it's your own incredibly unreasonable actions that force me to. I know how terribly you must feel but—damn it, man, postpone this going away! Face this situation like a man! Be reconciled to your child, stay with him at least until you can make suitable arrangements—

CURTIS—[Fixedly.] I will never see it! Never!

148

BIGELOW—How can you keep repeating that—with Martha hardly cold in her grave! I ask you again, what would she think, how would she feel—If you would only consent to see this baby, I know you'd realize how damnably mad and cruel you are. Won't you—just for a second?

CURTIS—No. [Then raging.] If I saw it I'd be tempted to—[Then brokenly.] No more of that talk, Big. I've heard enough. I've reached the limit.

BIGELOW—[Restraining his anger with difficulty—coldly.] That's your final answer, eh? Well, I'm through. I've done all I could. If you want to play the brute—to forget all that was most dear in the world to Martha—to go your own damn selfish way—well, there's nothing more to be said. You will be punished for it, believe me! [He takes a step toward the door.] And I—I want you to understand that all friendship ceases between us from this day. You are not the Curt I thought I knew—and I have nothing but a feeling of repulsion—good-by. [He starts for the door.]

CURTIS—[Dully.] Good-by, Big.

BIGELOW—[Stops, his features working with grief and looks back at his friend—then suddenly goes back to him—penitently.] Curt! Forgive me! I ought to know better. This isn't you. You'll come to yourself when you've had time to think it over. The memory of Martha—she'll tell you what you must do. [He wrings CURT's hand.] Good-by, old scout!

CURTIS—[Dully.] Good-by. [BIGELOW hurries out, rear. CURT sits in a dumb apathy for a while—then groans heart-brokenly.] Martha! Martha! [He springs to his feet distractedly. The door of the study is slowly opened and SHEFFIELD peers out cautiously—then comes into the room, followed by the others. They all take seats as before. CURT ignores them.]

SHEFFIELD—[Clearing his throat.] Curt—

CURTIS—[Suddenly.] What time is it, do you know!

149

SHEFFIELD—[Looking at his watch.] Two minutes to four.

CURTIS—[Impatiently.] Still an hour more of this!

JAYSON—[Clearing his throat.] Curt—[Before he starts what he intends to say, there is the sound of voices from the hall. ESTHER and LILY help in MRS. DAVIDSON to her former chair. The old lady's face is again transformed with joy. ESTHER joins EMILY on the couch. LILY sits in chair—front right. There is a long, uncomfortable pause during which CURT paces up and down.]

MRS. DAVIDSON—[Suddenly murmuring aloud to herself—happily.] He's such a dear! I could stay watching him forever.

JAYSON—[Testily.] Sshhh! Aunt! [Then clearing his throat again.] Surely you're not still thinking of going on the five o'clock train, are you, Curt?

CURTIS—Yes.

SHEFFIELD—[Drily.] Then Mr. Bigelow didn't persuade you—

CURTIS—[Coldly and impatiently.] I'm not to be persuaded by Big or anyone else. And I'll thank you not to talk any more about it. [They all stiffen resentfully at his tone.]

JAYSON—[To CURT—in a pleading tone.] You mustn't be unreasonable, Curt. After all we are your family—your best friends in the world—and we are only trying to help you—

CURTIS—[With nervous vehemence.] I don't want your help. You will help me most by keeping silent.

EMILY—[With a meaning look at the others—sneeringly.] Yes, no doubt.

ESTHER—Sshhh, Emily!

JAYSON—[Helplessly.] But, you see, Curt—

SHEFFIELD—[With his best judicial air.] If you'll all allow me to be

150

the spokesman, I think perhaps that I—[They all nod and signify their acquiescence.] Well, then, will you listen to me, Curt? [This last somewhat impatiently as CURT continues to pace, eyes on the floor.]

CURTIS—[Without looking at him—harshly.] Yes, I'm listening. What else can I do when you've got me cornered? Say what you like and let's get this over.

SHEFFIELD—First of all, Curt, I hope it is needless for me to express how very deeply we all feel for you in your sorrow. But we sincerely trust that you are aware of our heartfelt sympathy. [They all nod. A bitter, cynical smile comes over LILY's face.]

ESTHER—[Suddenly breaking down and beginning to weep.] Poor Martha! [SHEFFIELD glances at his wife, impatient at this interruption. The others also show their irritation.]

EMILY—[Pettishly.] Esther! For goodness sake! [CURT hesitates, stares at his sister frowningly as if judging her sincerity—then bends down over her and kisses the top of her bowed head impulsively—seems about to break down himself—grits his teeth and forces it back—glances around at the others defiantly and resumes his pacing. ESTHER dries her eyes, forcing a trembling smile. The cry has done her good.]

SHEFFIELD—[Clearing his throat.] I may truthfully say we all feel—as Esther does—even if we do not give vent—[With an air of sincere sympathy.] I know how terrible a day this must be for you, Curt. We all do. And we feel guilty in breaking in upon the sanctity of your sorrow in any way. But, if you will pardon my saying so, your own course of action—the suddenness of your plans—have made it imperative that we come to an understanding about certain things—about one thing in particular, I might say. [He pauses. CURT goes on pacing back and forth as if he hadn't heard.]

JAYSON—[Placatingly.] Yes, it is for the best, Curt.

ESTHER—Yes, Curt dear, you mustn't be unreasonable.

151

DICK—[Feeling called upon to say something.] Yes, old man, you've got to face things like a regular. Facts are facts. [This makes everybody uneasy.]

LILY—[Springing to her feet.] Phew! it's close in here. I'm going out in the garden. You can call me when these—orations—are finished. [She sweeps out scornfully.]

JAYSON—[Calling after her imperiously.] Lily! [But she doesn't answer and he gives it up with a hopeless sigh.]

CURTIS—[Harshly.] What time is it?

SHEFFIELD—You have plenty of time to listen to what I—I should rather say we—have to ask you, Curt. I promise to be brief. But first let me again impress upon you that I am talking in a spirit of the deepest friendliness and sympathy with you—as a fellow-member of the same family, I may say—and with the highest ideals and the honor of that family always in view. [CURT makes no comment. SHEFFIELD unconsciously begins to adopt the alert keenness of the cross-examiner.] First, let me ask you, is it your intention to take that five o'clock train to-day?

CURTIS—[Harshly.] I've told you that.

SHEFFIELD—And then you'll join this expedition to Asia?

CURTIS—You know that.

SHEFFIELD—To be gone five years?

CURTIS—[Shrugging his shoulders.] More or less.

SHEFFIELD—Is it your intention to return here at any time before you leave for Asia?

CURTIS—No!

SHEFFIELD—And your determination on these plans is irrevocable?

152

CURTIS—Irrevocable! Exactly. Please remember that.

SHEFFIELD—[Sharply.] That being your attitude, I will come bluntly to the core of the whole matter—the child whose coming into the world cost Martha her life.

CURTIS—[Savagely.] Her murderer! You are right! [They all look shocked, suspicious.]

SHEFFIELD—[Remonstratingly but suspiciously.] You can hardly hold the child responsible for the terrible outcome. Women die every day from the same cause. [Keenly.] Why do you attribute guilt to the child in this case, Curt?

CURTIS—It lives and Martha is gone—But, enough! I've said I never wanted it mentioned to me. Will you please remember that?

SHEFFIELD—[Sharply.] Its name is Jayson. Curt—in the eyes of the law. Will YOU please remember that?

CURTIS—[Distractedly.] I don't want to remember anything! [Wildly.] Please, for God's sake, leave me alone!

SHEFFIELD—[Coldly.] I am sorry, Curt, but you cannot act as if you were alone in this affair.

CURTIS—Why not? Am I not alone—more alone this minute than any creature on God's earth?

SHEFFIELD—[Soothingly.] In your great grief. Yes, yes, of course. We all appreciate—and we hate to—[Persuasively.] Yes, it would be much wiser to postpone these practical considerations until you are in a calmer mood. And if you will only give us the chance—why not put off this precipitate departure—for a month, say—and in the meantime—

CURTIS—[Harshly.] I am going when I said I was. I must get away from this horrible hole—as far away as I can. I must get back to my work for only in it will I find Martha again. But you—you can't

153

understand that. What is the good of all this talking which leads nowhere?

SHEFFIELD—[Coldly.] You're mistaken. It leads to this: Do you understand that your running away from this child—on the very day of its mother's funeral!—will have a very queer appearance in the eyes of the world?

EMILY—And what are you going to do with the baby, Curt? Do you think you can run off regardless and leave it here—on our hands?

CURTIS—[Distractedly.] I'll give it this home. And someone—anyone—Esther, Lily—can appoint a nurse to live here and—[Breaking down.] Oh, don't bother me!

SHEFFIELD—[Sharply.] In the world's eyes, it will appear precious like a desertion on your part.

CURTIS—Oh, arrange it to suit yourselves—anything you wish—

SHEFFIELD—[Quickly.] I'll take you at your word. Then let us arrange it this way. You will remain here a month longer at least—

CURTIS—No!

SHEFFIELD—[Ignoring the interruption.] You can make plans for the child's future in that time, become reconciled to it—

CURTIS—No!

JAYSON—[Pleadingly.] Curt—please—for all our sakes—when the honor of the family is at stake.

DICK—Yes, old man, there's that about it, you know.

CURTIS—No!

EMILY—Oh, he's impossible!

SHEFFIELD—Perhaps Curt misunderstood me. [Meaningly.] Be

reconciled to it in the eyes of the public, Curt. That's what I meant. Your own private feelings in the matter—are no one's business but your own, of course.

CURTIS—[Bewilderedly.] But—I don't see—Oh, damn your eyes of the public!

EMILY—[Breaking in.] It's all very well for you to ignore what people in town think—you'll be in China or heaven knows where. The scandal won't touch you—but we've got to live here and have our position to consider.

CURTIS—[Mystified.] Scandal? What scandal? [Then with a harsh laugh.] Oh, you mean the imbecile busy-bodies will call me an unnatural father. Well, let them! I suppose I am. But they don't know—

EMILY—[Spitefully.] Perhaps they know more than you think they do.

CURTIS—[Turning on her—sharply.] Just what do you mean by that, eh?

ESTHER—Emily! Shhh!

JAYSON—[Flurriedly.] Be still, Emily. Let Mark do the talking.

SHEFFIELD—[Interposing placatingly.] What Emily means is simply this, Curt: You haven't even been to look at this child since it has been born—not once, have you?

CURTIS—No, and I never intend—

SHEFFIELD—[Insinuatingly.] And don't you suppose the doctors and nurses—and the servants—have noticed this? It is not the usual procedure, you must acknowledge, and they wouldn't be human if they didn't think your action—or lack of action—peculiar and comment on it outside.

CURTIS—Well, let them! Do you think I care a fiddler's curse how people judge me?

155

SHEFFIELD—It is hardly a case of their judging—you. [Breaking off as he catches CURT'S tortured eyes fixed on him wildly.] This is a small town, Curt, and you know as well as I do, gossip is not the least of its faults. It doesn't take long for such things to get started. [Persuasively.] Now I ask you frankly, is it wise to provoke deliberately what may easily be set at rest by a little—I'll be frank— a little pretense on your part?

JAYSON—Yes, my boy. As a Jayson, I know you don't wish—

ESTHEE—[With a sigh.] Yes, you really must think of us, Curt.

CURTIS—[In an acute state of muddled confusion.] But—I—you— how are you concerned? Pretense? You mean you want me to stay and pretend—in order that you won't be disturbed by any silly tales they tell about me? [With a wild laugh.] Good God, this is too much! Why does a man have to be maddened by fools at such a time! [Raging.] Leave me alone! You're like a swarm of poisonous flies.

JAYSON—Curt! This is—really—when we've tried to be so considerate—

JOHN—[Bursting with rage.] It's an outrage to allow such insults!

DICK—You're not playing the game, Curt.

EMILY—[Spitefully.] It seems to me it's much more for Martha's sake, we're urging you than for our own. After all, the town can't say anything against us.

CURTIS—[Turning on her.] Martha's sake? [Brokenly.] Martha is gone. Leave her out of this.

SHEFFIELD—[Sharply.] But unfortunately, Curt, others will not leave her out of this. They will pry and pry—you know what they are—and—

EMILY—Curt couldn't act the way he is doing if he ever really cared for her.

CURTIS—You dare to say that! [Then controlling himself a bit—with scathing scorn.] What do know of love—women like you! You call your little rabbit-hutch emotions love—your bread-and-butter passions—and you have the effrontery to judge—

EMILY—[Shrinking from him frightenedly.] Oh! John!

JOHN—[Getting to his feet.] I protest! I cannot allow even my own brother—

DICK—[Grabbing his arm.] Keep your head, old boy.

SHEFFIELD—[Peremptorily.] You are making a fool of yourself, Curt—and you are damned insulting in the bargain. I think I may say that we've all about reached the end of our patience. What Emily said is for your own best interest, if you had the sense to see it. And I put it to you once and for all: Are you or are you not willing to act like a man of honor to protect your own good name, the family name, the name of this child, and your wife's memory? Let me tell you, your wife's good name is more endangered by your stubbornness than anything else.

CURTIS—[Trembling with rage.] I—I begin to think—you—all of you—are aiming at something against Martha in this. Yes—in back of your words—your actions—I begin to feel—[Raging.] Go away! Get out of this house—all of you! Oh, I know your meanness! I've seen how you've tried to hurt her ever since we came—because you resented in your small minds her evident superiority—

EMILY—[Scornfully.] Superiority, indeed!

CURTIS—Her breadth, of mind and greatness of soul that you couldn't understand. I've guessed all this, and if I haven't interfered it's only because I knew she was too far above you to notice your sickening malice—

EMILY—[Furiously.] You're only acting—acting for our benefit because you think we don't—

CURTIS—[Turning on her—with annihilating contempt.] Why,

157

you—you poor little nonentity! [John struggles to get forward but Dick holds him back.]

EMILY—[Insane with rage—shrilly.] But we know—and the whole town knows—and you needn't pretend you've been blind. You've given the whole thing away yourself—the silly way you've acted—telling everyone how you hated that baby—letting everyone see—

JAYSON—Emily! [The others are all frightened, try to interrupt her. CURT stares at her in a stunned bewilderment]

EMILY—[Pouring forth all her venom regardless.] But you might as well leave off your idiotic pretending. It doesn't fool us—or anyone else—your sending for Bigelow that night—your hobnobbing with him ever since—your pretending he's as much your friend as ever. They're all afraid of you—but I'm not! I tell you to your face—it's all acting you're doing—just cheap acting to try and pull the wool over our eyes until you've run away like a coward—and left us to face the disgrace for you with this child on our hands!

ESTHER—[Trying to silence her—excitedly.] Emily! Keep still, for Heaven's sake! [The others all utter exclamations of caution, with fearful glances at CURT.]

EMILY—[Becoming exhausted by her outburst—more faintly.] Well, someone had to show him his place. He thinks he's so superior to us just because—telling us how much better she was than—But I won't stand for that. I've always had a clean name—and always will—and my children, too, thank God! [She sinks down on the couch exhausted, panting but still glaring defiantly at CURT.]

CURTIS—[An awareness of her meaning gradually forcing itself on his mind.] Bigelow! Big? Pretending he's as much my friend—[With a sudden gasp of sickened understanding.] Oh! [He sways as if he were about to fall, shrinking away from EMILY, all horror.] Oh, you—you—you-filth!

JOHN—[His fists clenched, tries to advance on his brother.] How

158

dare you insult my wife! [He is restrained, held bake by his remonstrating father and DICK.]

MRS. DAVIDSON—[As if suddenly coming out of a dream—frightenedly.] What is the matter? Why is John mad at Curt?

CURTIS—[His hands over his eyes, acting like a person stricken with a sudden attack of nausea, weakly.] So—that's—what has been in your minds. Oh, this is bestial—disgusting! And there is nothing to be done. I feel defenseless. One would have to be as low as you are—She would have been defenseless, too. It is better she is dead. [He stares about him—wildly.] And you think—you all think—

ESTHER—[Pityingly.] Curt, dear, we don't think anything except what you've made us think with your crazy carrying-on.

CURTIS—[Looking from one to the other of them.] Yes—all of you—it's on your faces. [His eyes fix themselves on his aunt.] No, you don't—you don't—

MRS. DAVIDSON—I? Don't what, Curtis? My, how sick you look, poor boy!

CURTIS—You—don't believe—this child—

MRS. DAVIDSON—He's the sweetest baby I ever saw [proudly] and Jayson right to the tips of his toes.

CURTIS—Ah, I know you—[Looking around at the others with loathing and hatred.] But look at them—[With a burst of fierce determination.] Wait! I'll give you the only answer—[He dashes for the door in rear, shakes off his father and DICK, who try to stop him, and then is heard bounding up the stairs in hall. DICK runs after him, JAYSON as far as the doorway. ESTHER gives a stifled scream. There is a tense pause. Then DICK reappears.]

DICK—It's all right. I saw him go in.

JAYSON—[Frightenedly.] But—good God—he's liable—why didn't you follow him?

DICK—The doctor and nurse are there. They would have called out, wouldn't they, if—

MRS. DAVIDSON—[Getting angrier and angrier as her puzzlement has grown greater—in a stern tone.] I understand less and less of this. Where has Curtis gone? Why did he act so sick? What is the matter with all of you?

ESTHER—Nothing, Aunt dear, nothing!

MRS. DAVIDSON—No, you'll not hush me up! [Accusingly.] You all look guilty. Have you been saying anything against Curtis' baby? That was what Curtis seemed to think. A fine time you've picked out—with his wife not cold in her grave!

JAYSON—Aunt!

MRS. DAVIDSON—I never liked that woman. I never understood her. But now—now I love her and beg her forgiveness. She died like a true woman in the performance of her duty. She died gloriously— and I will always respect her memory. [Suddenly flying into a passion.] I feel that you are all hostile to her baby—poor, little, defenseless creature! Yes, you'd hate the idea of Curtis' having a son—you and your girls! Well, I'll make you bitterly regret the day you—[She plumps herself down in her chair again, staring stubbornly and angrily before her.]

EMILY—[Spitefully.] I fear it will be necessary to tell Aunt—

JAYSON—Sshh! You have made enough trouble with your telling already! [Miserably.] It should never have come to this pass. Curt will never forgive us, never!

ESTHER—[Resentfully to EMILY.] See what not holding your tongue has done—and my children will have to suffer for it, too!

SHEFFIELD—[Severely.] If Emily had permitted me to conduct this business uninterruptedly, this would never have occurred.

EMILY—That's right! All pick on me! Cowards! [She breaks down and sobs.]

160

DICK—[From the doorway. Coming back into the room.] Sstt! Here he comes!

CURTIS—[Reenters. There is a look of strange exultation on his face. He looks from one to the other of them. He stammers.] Well—my answer to you—your rotten world—I kissed him—he is mine! He looked at me—it was as if Martha looked at me—through his eyes.

ESTHER—[Voicing the general relief. Joyfully.] Oh, Curt! You won't go now? You'll stay?

CURTIS—[Staring at her, then from one to another of the rest with a withering scorn.] Ha! Now you think you have conquered, do you? No, I'm not going to stay! Do you think your vile slander could influence me to give up my work? And neither shall you influence the life of my son. I leave him here. I must. But not to your tender mercies. No, no! Thank God, there still remains one Jayson with unmuddled integrity to whom I can appeal. [He goes to MRS. DAVIDSON.] I will leave him in your care, Aunt—while I am gone.

MRS. DAVIDSON—[Delighted.] It will be a great happiness. He will be—the one God never granted me. [Her lips trembling.] God has answered my prayer at last.

CURTIS—I thank you, Aunt. [Kisses her reverentially.]

MRS. DAVIDSON—[Pleased but morally bound to grumble at him] But I cannot approve of your running away like this. It isn't natural. [Then with selfish haste, fearing her words may change his mind and she will lose the baby.] But you always were a queer person—and a man must do faithfully the work ordained for him.

CURTIS—[Gladly.] Yes, I must go! What would I be for him—or anyone—if I stayed? Thank God, you understand. But I will come back. [The light of an ideal beginning to shine in his eyes.] When he is old enough, I will teach him to know and love a big, free life. Martha used to say that he would take her part in time. My goal shall be his goal, too. Martha shall live again for me in him. And you, Aunt, swear to keep him with you—out there in the country—never to let him know this obscene little world. [He indicates his relatives.]

MRS. DAVIDSON—Yes, I promise, Curtis. Let anyone dare—! [She glares about her. The noise of a motor is heard from the drive. It stops in front of the house.]

CURTIS—I must go. [He kisses his aunt.] Teach him his mother was the most beautiful soul that ever lived. Good-by, Aunt.

MRS. DAVIDSON—Good-by, Curtis! [Without looking at the others, he starts for the door, rear. They all break out into conscience-stricken protestations.]

JAYSON—[Miserably.] Curt! You're not leaving us that way?

ESTHER—Curt—you're going—without a word! [They all say this practically together and crowd toward him. JOHN and EMILY remain sullenly apart. CURT turns to face them.]

LILY—[Enters from the rear.] You're not going, Curt?

CURTIS—[Turning to her.] Yes. Good-by, Lily. [He kisses her.] You loved her, didn't you? You are not like—Take my advice and get away before you become—[He has been staring into her face. Suddenly he pushes her brusquely away from him—coldly.] But I see in your face it's too late.

LILY—[Miserably.] No, Curt—I swear—

CURTIS—[Facing them all defiantly.] Yes, I am going without a word—because I cannot find the fitting one. Be thankful I can't. It would shrivel up your souls like flame, [He again turns and strides to the door.]

JAYSON—[His grief overcoming him.] My boy! We are wrong—we know—but—at least say you forgive us.

CURTIS—[Wavers with his back towards them—then turns and

162

forces the words out.] Ask forgiveness of her. She—yes—she was so fine—I feel she—so you are forgiven. Good-by. [He goes. The motor is heard driving off. There is a tense pause.]

LILY—Then he did find out? Oh, a fine mess you've made of everything! But no—I should say "we," shouldn't I? Curt guessed that. Oh, I hate you—and myself! [She breaks down.]

[There is a strained pause during which they are all silent, their eyes avoiding each other, fixed in dull, stupid stares. Finally, DICK fidgets uncomfortably, heaves a noisy sigh, and blurts out with an attempt at comforting reassurance:]

DICK—Well, it isn't as bad as it might have been, anyway. He did acknowledge the kid—before witnesses, too.

JAYSON—[Testily.] Keep your remarks to yourself, if you please! [But most of his family are already beginning to look relieved.]

[The Curtain Falls]

9 781636 379357